CROW AND RIDER

AN IRON WAY NOVEL

By Max Sterling

Based on the Iron Way setting created by C. Holtorf

Distributed by Smokeshow Publishing

CHAPTER 1: THE SCORE AND THE SIGN

The grit of the I-25 corridor was a taste Phillip Tweese knew intimately. It coated his tongue, settled in the lines around his eyes, and dusted the worn shoulders of his patched canvas jacket. He'd been walking for three days since leaving that last dusty settlement – what was its name? Purgatoire, or something equally forgettable – with a little more in his pack than when he'd arrived, and a distinct lack of farewell pleasantries. The "water purification" tablets he'd traded (mostly charcoal and hope, if he was honest) had probably stopped working by now, if they ever had. Best not to linger on such details. The point was, he'd eaten well for a few days, and his pack, while lighter now, wasn't entirely empty. Yet. He needed to keep moving, put some miles between himself and any lingering resentment. North, south, it hardly mattered, as long as it was away.

Trinidad. The faded, sun-bleached sign on the outskirts of the ruin was barely legible, its letters pocked with rust and what looked suspiciously like buckshot. Another ghost town whispering of the long decline, another collection of picked-over bones for scavengers like him to gnaw on. His supplies were dwindling again, the familiar ache of hunger a dull counterpoint to the weariness in his legs. He needed to find something, anything, to replenish his stock before pushing on. Hope, as he often reminded himself, was a thin gruel, but a score, a real find, that could change things.

He moved with the cautious, practiced gait of a man who knew that silence and observation were his best allies. The streets of Trinidad were choked with debris, the skeletal remains of buildings slumped like weary giants. Nature was slowly, stubbornly reclaiming its territory, weeds pushing through cracked asphalt, and hardy, scrubby bushes taking root in the crevices of crumbling brickwork. It wasn't a place to linger, especially not when making enough noise to attract every other desperate soul who might be lurking in the shadows. He'd learned long ago that the most dangerous predators in this new world walked on two legs.

His eyes, sharp and constantly scanning, darted from shadowed doorways to collapsed rooftops, assessing potential threats, potential opportunities. A glint of metal here, a patch of undisturbed dust there – the subtle language of the ruins. He was a crow, picking through the leavings of a dead world, his moral compass a flexible, pragmatic thing, bent by the constant, grinding necessity of survival. Right and wrong were luxuries few could afford. Staying alive, that was the only commandment that truly mattered.

He'd made his way south along the crumbling spine of what they still called the I-25, a ribbon of cracked asphalt and rusted-out vehicles, talking quickly through any encounter with his fellow scavs, his mind always calculating. It's just how it was, he figured. It's how it'd been for as long as anyone could remember, or at least for as long as the stories passed down from grandparents to grandchildren could recall: You either found what you needed to live, or you took it from the guy who wasn't fast enough to get away, or smart enough to talk you out of it. Tweese prided himself on being both fast and smart, though he preferred the latter. Violence was messy, unpredictable. A well-placed word, a carefully constructed bluff, that was an art form. An art form that had served him well in Purgatoire, at least until his welcome had worn decidedly thin.

The old world had ended not with a sudden bang, nor even a protracted, screaming war that folk still whispered tales of, but with a slow, grinding cessation of all the things that had once made it function. Bad governance, they said, if anyone bothered to say anything at all about how things got this way. The climate had gone feral, like a starved dog turning on its master. Systems, intricate and fragile as a spider's web, had simply frayed and then snapped, one by one, until the whole tapestry of what was had unraveled into the what-is. Phillip Tweese, like most everyone born in the century since the worst of it, knew this less as history and more as the texture of the air he breathed.

A flicker of something less decayed caught his eye. A husk of a building just a little less ravaged, tucked away down a side street littered with the rusted husks of ancient vehicles. JM Tires, a faded sign above a partially collapsed doorway proclaimed, its letters peeling like sunburnt skin. Most garages were picked clean within years of the Collapse, but this one looked… slightly less violated. Maybe. Or maybe it was just another dead end. But his dwindling supplies, and the memory of that too-quick departure from Purgatoire, urged him forward. He needed a score, and soon.

He'd found the old thing in the grey pre-dawn, a pale ghost wrapped in layers of heavy, oil-stained canvas, nestled deep in the cracked and web-choked bay of that very garage. The motorcycle – for that's what he eventually realized it was – lay entombed in the monkey pit, that narrow concrete trench where mechanics of a bygone era, an era of plentiful oil and roaring engines, would have crawled beneath vehicles to coax them back to life. Back when there were cars worth coaxing. Back when "mechanic" was a profession one could aspire to, rather than a quaint, archaic term for someone who might, if you were lucky, know how to patch a tire or splice a wire.

Hell, at first, squinting into the gloom of the pit, kicking aside rusted tools and the desiccated husks of unidentifiable creatures, Tweese wasn't even sure what the canvas-shrouded lump was. An engine, perhaps, given the locale. A generator, maybe, though it seemed too long, too oddly shaped. Honestly, if it hadn't been so meticulously wrapped, cocooned against the slow decay that claimed everything else in this dead corner of Trinidad, he probably would have left it. Scavenging was a game of percentages, of energy expended versus potential gain. Digging out a heavy, unknown object from a collapsed pit, alone, was usually a fool's errand. But sometimes you got lucky. Sometimes the worthless-looking rock turned out to be a geode, glittering with unexpected treasure within. For Phillip Tweese, a man whose life was a testament to the art of sifting treasure from trash, today felt like one of those days. Or at least, he hoped it was.

It took most of the morning, a grueling, sweat-soaked, muscle-straining effort, just to get chains around the bulky object and rig it to the ancient, creaking cherry picker he'd found in the back of the garage. The hydraulic seals on the picker were shot, of course, leaking a dark, viscous fluid that smelled of time and regret, but with enough brute force on the pump handle, it still held a grudging pressure. Each rasp of the chain, each groan of the metal as he worked the hoist, echoed unnaturally loud in the oppressive silence of the ruined town. Trinidad was a skeletal reminder of how far things had fallen – buildings slumped like weary giants, streets choked with debris and the stubborn, reclaiming efforts of nature. It wasn't a place to linger, especially not when making enough noise to attract every desperate soul within earshot.

In fact, Tweese was expecting someone to show up and catch him with his metaphorical pants down the whole time he was working. His senses were stretched taut, every rustle of wind in the desiccated weeds, every distant clatter of dislodged rubble, setting his teeth on edge. It was a hell of a risk, a gamble played out in the open, but as the shrouded form finally cleared the lip of the pit, swinging precariously on the chains, the distinct shape of wheels beneath the canvas became clear. His breath hitched. It wasn't just an engine – it was a motorcycle! A complete motorcycle. His heart hammered against his ribs, a wild, frantic drumbeat of avarice and excitement.

He was hoping it still ran, the potential value of a working motorcycle leveraging itself heavily against the ever-present risk of getting caught too busy, too exposed, to fight back or flee. A working bike wasn't just a find; it was a life-altering prize. *This changes things,* he thought, a new, audacious idea sparking in his mind. *With this, I could go north. All the way to Cheyenne.* He knew the Iron Way, the almost mythical biker gang that patrolled the northern territories, would trade just about anything for a ride in this kind of condition – assuming the condition under the wraps was as good as the care taken in preserving it suggested. If he played his cards right, they might even trade him some land up Wyoming way, maybe a small plot along a river, a place where the earth was still black and fertile. Oh, he'd tithe, of course, just like any other sodbuster or smallholder under their protection. The Iron Way maintained a rough sort of order on their roads, cleared debris, dealt with raiders, and for that, they extracted their due. But was it really too much to ask that they let him enjoy the peace they'd carved out of the plains? Phil didn't think so. A patch of dirt, a roof that didn't leak, the quiet satisfaction of watching things grow – it was a dream so potent it almost made him careless.

He finally got the last of the stiff, grimy wrappings off just as the sun began its slow descent, painting the sky in hues of bruised purple and blood orange. Darkness was falling across the cracked concrete pad of JM Tires, or what was left of it. The place had been pretty well picked over long before Phil had ever found these ruins of Trinidad, another ghost town whispering of the long decline further south along the I-25. He'd learned to read the signs of a thoroughly scavenged location – the absence of anything easily portable, the systematic way in which walls were breached, floors torn up. JM Tires had been stripped bare, mostly. Mostly.

Even in the ever-dimming gloom, he could tell he'd found something truly special. The back wheel was large, its diameter more easily appreciated since the fender meant to cover its upper half had been chopped short, ending just a few inches past the rear lights. The lights themselves, twin red lozenges, were intact but painted over with thick black paint, leaving only the thinnest of crescent slits at their very bottoms. Tweese nodded to himself in approval; whoever had stored this bike here had expected trouble, had planned for it. The bike had been rigged to ride at night, as unobtrusively as possible. A ghost machine for a ghost world.

Considering how old it must be – easily over a hundred years, a relic from the full bloom of the Before Times – it was in remarkable shape. The chrome, where it peeked through a layer of dust, still held a deep, lustrous sheen. The paint, a dark, midnight blue, was faded in places but largely unmarred. Even the twin saddlebags, sleekly integrated into the upholstery of the second seat, looked to be in perfect condition. They were works of art, crafted from thick, supple black leather that felt alive beneath his calloused fingertips. They looked for all the world as if they had been made no more than a year ago, by a master of leatherworking whose skills had somehow survived the general decay of craft. The black surface had been embossed with intricate floral work, stylized roses at each corner with thorny vines connecting them in a delicate, dangerous border around the flap. A picture of a rearing horse, with two stylized, almost skeletal knights upon its back, had been embossed into the bottom center of each bag's flap. The toggle that held each flap closed, a burnished piece of brass, was cleverly shaped to form the cross on the first knight's shield.

Once he had it fully unwrapped and standing upright on its kickstand, he could see that it was a beautiful, brutal machine. A road cruiser, built for long, lonesome stretches of highway. The engine block nestled below the teardrop gas tank showed signs of custom work – polished fins, braided steel lines, a look of purposeful engineering that spoke of power and reliability. As Phil bent to take a better look, he whistled in low appreciation. Twin lines of sheathed and braided steel dropped from the tank to either side of the engine, held fast against the engine block by blued steel clips. A third line ran from the back of the tank, disappearing into the depths of the engine's guts. As Phil peered under the engine, he saw that these lines ran to some sort of complex wiring harness, tucked away neatly beneath the tank, shielded from the elements.

He prodded the gas tank gently with a knuckle. It felt solid, heavy. He rocked the bike slightly, and heard it – a distinct, liquid slosh from within. It still held fuel! Or, a more sobering thought immediately followed, I'll open it to find it full of water and rust, and the whole damned thing will be ruined. The way things had fallen apart, it was always a toss-up – dangling hope, then snatching it away with a cruel laugh. Shrugging to himself, a gesture of fatalistic acceptance he'd perfected over years of similar gambles, he stood up and gave the chromed gas cap a quarter turn. It resisted for a moment, then yielded with a soft hiss. As he lifted it, the acrid, chemical sting of old fuel filled his nose, but it was coupled with another, more organic, and surprisingly familiar scent... pork fat? Of course, he thought, replacing the cap once more. Bio-diesel.

It was another stroke of luck for Phil, a significant one. Though he doubted the fuel currently in the tank itself was still good after who knew how many decades, the fact that the bike was converted to run on biodiesel meant that finding more fuel was a realistic possibility. Rendered animal fats, certain types of processed vegetable matter – these were things that could still be scavenged, or even produced in some of the more stable settlements. He really could ride this thing to Cheyenne, if he played his cards right. And if the damned thing actually ran.

There was nothing for it but to give it a try. The sun had now fully sunk below the jagged silhouette of an old, collapsed auto-dealership across the street, plunging the garage into deep twilight. Phil knew that if it didn't start, he'd have to make a hard decision, and quickly. If he was going to try and fix it, it would have to wait till morning, and that would mean camping right here, in the middle of the ruins; never a good idea. Trinidad might be picked over, but it wasn't entirely empty. Desperate things, both animal and human, still slunk through its shadowed arteries. The only other option was to abandon the bike, try to hide it again, and maybe come back tomorrow. But he knew himself well enough. Once he got out of these ruins, he wouldn't come back. He never had before. You moved on. It was the cardinal rule that had kept him alive this long. Don't look back. Don't get attached. Don't linger.

He sighed, the sound a small, weary exhalation in the vast, uncaring silence. He turned his attention back to the saddlebags, running his hands over the embossed leather. He unlatched the right-side bag and thrust a hand in, casting about for keys. His fingers brushed against cold metal, then something hard and angular, then something soft. He pulled out three items, each incredibly valuable in its own right, though none of them were the keys he so desperately wanted.

The first was a .45 automatic pistol, its blackened metal cool and heavy in his palm. It was an old-world design, brutally efficient, its weight obvious to Phil even before he fully removed it from the bag. It felt good in his hand, a solid, reassuring presence. The second item was the weapon's magazine, though a quick check revealed it was empty; no bullets had been pushed into place within its steel lips. Not that the lack of bullets in the magazine made the gun entirely useless, though. The final item in the bag was a single, .45 caliber bullet. Just one. But it wasn't just any bullet. He recognized the color-coded tip, even in the fading light. Armor piercing. A round designed to punch through hardened targets, a statement of serious intent. One bullet. One chance to make a very big impression, or solve a very big problem.

The bag on the left side was stuffed full with a single, bulky item: a heavy leather jacket. Phil couldn't make out its details in the growing darkness, but he could tell by its sheer weight and the stiffness of the material that it was a quality piece of gear. As he pulled it free, he felt the tell-tale rigidity of protective panels sewn into the lining. Panels of hardened plastic, or perhaps even kinetic gel, formed cups at the elbows and shoulders, with more sewn into place strategically across the back and chest. *You could probably take more than just a fall from the bike in that,* Phil thought, a grim appreciation dawning. He thought about the coming cold of the high plains, the biting winds of the I-25 corridor. Its ability to potentially stop a bullet, or at least a knife thrust, paled in immediate worth compared to its more mundane ability to keep him warm. As he twisted it about, feeling for its zipper, the coat jingled softly, a tell-tale sign that something was nestled in its pockets. Changing his focus, he thrust his hands into the jacket's deep side pockets and almost cackled in glee as his right hand closed over a small, metallic ring holding a set of vehicle keys.

"Well, now," Tweese said, his voice a low murmur addressed to no one in particular, the words tasting of triumph on his tongue. He unzipped the jacket with a decisive tug and shrugged it on in one smooth motion. It was heavy, reassuringly so, and smelled faintly of leather, old engine oil, and something else... a faint, almost metallic tang, like ozone after a lightning strike. "Let's see if this dream has wings."

He lifted one leg up and over the bike, straddling it, the cool leather of the seat molding to him. He grabbed the wide-set handlebars, feeling the worn texture of the grips beneath his palms. He shifted the bike's weight off its stand and settled into the seat. It was surprisingly comfortable, the seat well-cushioned, its shape designed so that the rise of the second rider's seat formed a perfect, cushioned support for his lower back. He could even lean back slightly and let it take his weight. To make a long trip even easier, a set of folding highway pegs rested near the hub of the front wheel. The forks of the bike were canted so that they flung far forward, putting these pegs at a perfect, almost reclining height for his feet. *The damn bike might as well have been made for me,* he thought, a surge of possessiveness, of belonging, washing over him. *It's perfect for riding the highway, long distance. Built for the endless, broken ribbon of the I-25.*

With a tremor of trepidation in his heart, a fear that this was all too good to be true, that the dream would shatter at the last moment, he put the key in the ignition, located just below the handlebars on the side of the steering column. He turned it to the 'on' indicator. A single, dim red light flickered to life on the minimalist dashboard. Then, holding his breath, he thumbed the starter button.

For a heart-stopping second, nothing happened. Then, a slow, hesitant churn. The diesel engine began to choke, to cough, then, with a surprisingly subdued series of chuffs, it rumbled into life. The engine didn't roar the way he'd expected a bike of this size to. Instead, it settled into a fast, rhythmic thumping heartbeat, a powerful but muted pulse. He imagined the conversion to diesel, and whatever other modifications had been made for stealth, probably robbed the bike of some of its raw horsepower, but the resulting engine ran significantly more quietly than anything Phil had encountered before that wasn't powered by muscle or wind.

This bike... this bike might be worth a lot more to the Iron Way than I initially thought! The realization hit him with the force of a physical blow, sending a wave of pure, unadulterated glee coursing through him. This wasn't just a ticket to a piece of land; this was a masterpiece of post-collapse engineering, a ghost in the machine perfectly suited to this dangerous, depleted world.

Phil was riding that wave, grinning like a madman. He kicked up the bike's stand with a satisfying clang. With his left hand, he pulled in the clutch lever; it was stiff but smooth. He tapped the shifter down with his left foot, feeling the solid click as the bike engaged its lowest gear. Then, slowly, carefully, he began to let out the clutch with one hand while simultaneously twisting the throttle grip on the right handlebar with the other.

The bike shot forward with an unexpected surge of torque, dragging his right foot across the broken concrete before he could snatch it up and place it on its peg. He wrestled with the sudden power for a moment, his grin widening into a rictus of exhilaration and mild panic. Still, the bike was running! It was alive! His face split with that grin as he flicked on the bike's lights – or what passed for them.

The front headlight, like the rear ones, had been almost entirely painted over. Only a small, narrow slit at its lower half remained uncovered, casting a low, focused beam of pale yellow light across the ground directly ahead of him. It was just enough to see the immediate road surface, the rubble, the potholes. He realized it was also a lot easier on his night vision, allowing him to see into the deeper shadows beyond the beam's reach.

It never occurred to him, not then, in that first flush of triumph, to wonder *why* the bike seemed so perfectly, so professionally, suited to stealthily traveling the ruined roads. Or who might have possessed the skills and resources to create such a machine, and why they might have abandoned it. Phil was on his way, and for now, that was all that mattered.

His high, that intoxicating cocktail of adrenaline and elation, lasted for about twenty glorious minutes. He navigated the bike out of the skeletal remains of Trinidad, the quiet thrum of its engine a comforting counterpoint to the desolate silence of the dead town. Once he hit the relatively open expanse of the I-25 northbound, he couldn't resist. He gunned the engine, wanting to see what the bike could really do. It was faster than he expected, the acceleration smooth and powerful, eating up the miles of broken highway with an easy grace. But it also ate through its meager supply of ancient, congealed biodiesel with an alarming appetite.

With a final, sputtering belch of greasy, bacon-scented smoke, the engine puttered to a halt. He coasted for a hundred yards in sudden, unwelcome silence, the only sound the crunch of tires on loose gravel as he steered the now-inert machine onto the crumbling shoulder. He was, if the faded and bullet-riddled road sign still standing drunkenly nearby was to be believed, about five miles from a town called Walsenberg. Or Watsenberg. Or... Actually, Phil wasn't sure exactly what the name of the town was. Most of the official lettering on the highway sign proclaiming the town's existence, including its name, had been crudely painted over in hand-scrawled script of stark white paint that read:

THE LORD PROVIDES FOR THE FAITHFUL, THE RIGHTEOUS AND THE MEEK

All of it in letters a foot tall if they were an inch. As he began the arduous task of pushing the heavy motorcycle in the deepening darkness, the silence of the plains pressing in on him, he hoped, with a fervor that surprised him, that the sign was right. Because Phillip Tweese, his dreams of Cheyenne and a riverside plot of land momentarily evaporating like morning mist, felt pretty damned meek compared to how he had felt just a few minutes earlier. The way the world was now, it always seemed to find a way to have the last laugh.

Phil figured he'd covered more than thirty miles in the short time he'd been riding, the landscape a blur of decaying infrastructure and the vast, indifferent emptiness of the plains. The remaining five miles to the town of Whatsitberg, on the other hand? That took him nearly three soul-crushing hours. The whole time, the bike, his glorious prize, seemed to grow heavier and harder to push with each trudging, doleful step. The initial elation had long since curdled into a grim, sweaty determination, fueled by dwindling hope and the gnawing ache in his muscles.

As the "city" – a generous term for the collection of dark, silent structures huddled in the distance – finally came into view, Phil's heart didn't get any lighter. From this vantage point, it looked as dark and deserted as any of the other hollowed-out cities of the time before. No welcoming lights, no plumes of smoke indicating hearths and homes. *No one lived here,* he thought with a sinking feeling, *at least no one who looked like they might "provide for the meek."* More likely, if anyone *was* here, they'd be the kind to prey on the meek, stripping them of anything valuable before leaving them for the coyotes.

Cursing under his breath – a litany of inventive and increasingly desperate profanities – he eased the weight of the bike down the crumbling offramp and into the city itself. He tucked it back behind the massive concrete support pillar of the overpass, hoping it would be out of sight from the main road. He had to admit, with a fresh wave of self-recrimination, that he hadn't expected he'd need fuel so soon. He'd been so caught up in the fantasy of a quick ride to Cheyenne that practicalities like fuel consumption had been an afterthought. Now, the idea that he could get this massive, beautiful hunk of metal all the way to Wyoming seemed like pure, unadulterated folly.

He looked around in the oppressive gloom, the silence broken only by the sigh of the wind through broken windows and the distant, mournful howl of a dog – or perhaps something less domesticated. What to do next? The chances he'd just stumble upon some ready-to-use bio-diesel in a town abandoned for so long seemed infinitesimally slim, at best. From the sign on the highway, he'd been half-hoping he'd find some sort of religious commune, a pocket of resilient believers still rendering fat or pressing oil. Someplace he could trade a few hours of labor, or perhaps some of the scavenged trinkets he carried in his pack, for a gallon or two of fuel. Now, it was pretty clear that Whatsitberg wasn't that place. It was just another corpse in the graveyard of the old world.

Or... was it?

Assuming that his first, bleak assessment of the town being yet another dead ruin was correct, Phil was utterly unprepared for the sight of the Walsenberg Court House as he cautiously rounded the corner onto what must have once been the town's main street. At first, he thought its hulking marble expanse, ghostly pale in the moonlight, was abandoned like everything else. Its windows were dark, its massive doors closed. But then, from a block away, his scavenger's eyes, honed by years of peering into shadows, began to make out indistinct forms. Shapes that resolved themselves, as he drew a little closer, into the unmistakable silhouettes of guards. Two of them, maybe three, standing on the courthouse's broad marble stairs, near the main entrance, their stillness somehow more menacing than movement would have been. They weren't just standing; they were watching.

He began to wonder what they could possibly be guarding in a place like this, when a flicker of movement caught his eye. A curtain, or perhaps a ragged piece of cloth serving as one, was pulled back from a high window on the second floor of the courthouse. For a brief moment, a blazing, warm light spilled out into the night, and framed within it, the small, innocent face of a young boy, peering intently into the darkness. The boy was clearly looking for something, or someone. Phil's stomach tightened. He realized, with a jolt of unease that had nothing to do with his aching muscles, that it must mean they knew he was here. They knew he was already in their town.

It was always tense, this moment, when you came upon other people in the ruins. Even more so when those people were actively squatting, claiming a piece of the dead world as their own. You never knew if they were just trying to scratch out a life in the concrete corpses of the past, struggling for the same meager resources as you, or if they were looking for some more direct, more concrete gain by making you and yours into fresh corpses, easily looted. The line between survivor and predator was often vanishingly thin.

"That's far enough, stranger." The voice, rough and wary, called out from the darkness ahead of him, from the direction of the courthouse steps. Before Phil could focus his eyes in the gloom, before he could even think to raise a placating hand, he was overcome by the sudden, blinding glare of a lantern as its shutter was thrown open and it was held high, its beam pinning him like an insect.

He winced at the unexpected assault of light, instinctively throwing up a hand to shade his eyes. For a moment, all he could see were dancing spots. Then, as his vision slowly cleared, the lantern light still masked nearly everything about its holder, save for the ragged, dark-cuffed denim of a pair of old-world jeans and the glint of what might have been a weapon held low at their side.

The lantern's glare was a physical force, pressing against Tweese's eyeballs, making them ache. He blinked, trying to dispel the swimming spots of light, his hand still half-raised. The silence stretched, taut and brittle, broken only by the faint, rhythmic creak of the lantern's handle as its unseen bearer shifted their weight. Behind the blinding corona, Tweese could sense, more than see, other figures moving, coalescing in the gloom on the courthouse steps. The night air, already cold, seemed to drop another few degrees, prickling his skin.

"I said, that's far enough," the voice repeated, a low growl that held a tremor of something Tweese couldn't quite place – fear, perhaps, or maybe just the bone-deep weariness of a man who'd seen too much trouble. "Who are you? What's your business in Walsenberg?"

Tweese lowered his hand slowly, letting his eyes adjust. The figure holding the lantern resolved into a burly man, his face a mask of shadow beneath the wide brim of a battered hat. The glint of metal Tweese had seen was indeed a weapon – a sawn-off shotgun, held loosely but purposefully at his side. Two other men flanked him, equally shadowed, equally armed with makeshift weapons – a heavy pipe wrench in one's grasp, a sharpened length of rebar in the other's. Settlers. Wary, desperate, and by the looks of them, not eager to welcome strangers. Standard.

"Name's Phil," Tweese said, keeping his voice even, trying for a tone of weary traveler rather than cornered scavenger. "Just passing through. Bike ran out of fuel a few miles back. Was hoping to find a place to rest, maybe trade for a little go-juice." He jerked a thumb vaguely over his shoulder, towards the overpass where his prize lay hidden. No need to advertise its presence just yet.

The lantern bearer took a step forward, the light bobbing. "Bike, you say?" His voice was skeptical. "Ain't many folks riding bikes these days. 'Specially not ones that need 'go-juice' instead of leg-power."

Another voice, thinner and more nervous, piped up from the shadows behind the first man. "Look at his jacket, Jed. And he's a big fella. Could be... could be one of *them*."

Jed, the lantern bearer, didn't turn, but Tweese saw his head tilt slightly, as if considering the words. One of *them*. The phrase hung in the air. Tweese felt a familiar prickle of calculation, the grifter's instinct stirring. He was wearing the heavy, armored leather jacket he'd found with the motorcycle. It was impressive, even in the dim, flickering light. And the bike itself, though currently out of sight, was a machine of undeniable quality and presence. *These folks seem ready to believe something,* he thought. *Let's see what that something is.*

"Step into the light, Phil," Jed commanded, his voice a fraction less hostile, a fraction more... curious? Or was it apprehension? "Let's have a proper look at you."

Tweese hesitated for a heartbeat. This was the pivot point. He could try to bluff his way through as a simple scavenger, down on his luck. Or... He thought of the jacket, the bike, the almost reverential tone in the nervous man's voice. *One of them.* He knew who "they" likely meant. The Iron Way. Their reputation, a mixture of fear and respect, extended far south, even into these forgotten corners. This could be useful. Very useful.

He took a slow, deliberate step forward, emerging more fully into the lantern's glow. He let the jacket hang open slightly, revealing nothing but his own worn shirt beneath, but allowing its bulk and protective panels to be more evident. He stood tall, trying to project an air of quiet confidence, of someone accustomed to being in charge, to being looked at. He'd played many roles in his life; this one felt like it might have some real leverage.

There was a collective intake of breath from the men on the steps. The nervous one muttered something incoherent. Even Jed seemed to straighten up a little.

"That's... that's an Iron Way jacket, ain't it?" Jed's voice was softer now, the suspicion tinged with something akin to awe, or perhaps just a more profound level of caution. "And the bike you mentioned... one of their cruisers?"

Tweese let a slow, almost imperceptible nod be his answer. He didn't confirm, didn't deny. He let them fill in the blanks, their imaginations, fueled by desperation and rumor, doing the work for him. It was a classic grifter's ploy: say little, suggest much. *They're writing the script themselves,* he mused. *Easiest con I've stumbled into in years.*

"We... we ain't seen an Iron Way rider this far south in... well, in a long time," Jed continued, his shotgun now held a little less aggressively, though still present. "Thought you boys kept mostly to the northern roads, up past Denver."

"Roads change. Times change," Tweese said, his voice deliberately low and gravelly, hoping it sounded like someone who'd spent years with engine roar and windburn as his constant companions. He was improvising, walking a tightrope, but the settlers' reaction was a clear tell. He could feel the shift in their posture, the subtle easing of tension, replaced by a kind of fearful deference. This deference was a tool, a key. It could open doors, loosen tongues, and, most importantly, secure resources.

"You alone?" Jed asked, his eyes flicking past Tweese, trying to pierce the darkness of the street.

"For now," Tweese replied, letting the implication hang. *Let them wonder. A little fear keeps people compliant.*

The men on the steps exchanged uneasy glances. The one with the pipe wrench licked his lips. The child who had been peeking from the courthouse window had reappeared, his small face pressed against the grimy pane, eyes wide.

"Look," Jed said, his tone shifting again, becoming almost pleading. "If you're Iron Way... we don't mean no trouble. None at all. This here's Walsenberg. We're just simple folk, trying to get by."

Simple folk trying to get by. Tweese had heard that line a thousand times. It usually preceded a request, or a demand, or an attempt to get something for nothing. But this time, the desperation in Jed's voice was a live current. They weren't just wary; they were scared. And they saw him – or the illusion he was projecting – as powerful. That power could be his shield and his ticket.

"We... we got a little trouble of our own, truth be told," Jed admitted, his gaze dropping for a moment before meeting Tweese's again. "Maybe... maybe someone like you could help. If you were so inclined. We'd make it worth your while, of course. Food. Fuel for your machine. Whatever we got."

Tweese's mind raced. This was it. The hook. They were offering him exactly what he needed: food, fuel, shelter. All he had to do was maintain the charade. It was almost too easy. He saw the hope flickering in Jed's eyes, the way the other men leaned forward. They were desperate for a solution, any solution, and they'd already decided he was it. The stories about the Iron Way – protectors, enforcers – were working for him.

The risks were there, of course. Impersonating the Iron Way was playing with fire. If they found out, or if real riders appeared, things could get ugly fast. But the immediate rewards were too tempting to ignore. Food. Fuel. A safe place to lie low for a night. And all it cost was a little play-acting. For a man of his talents, it was a bargain. The respect they were showing him wasn't a "heady brew" for his ego; it was a tactical advantage, a sign of their gullibility and his leverage.

He let the silence draw out, then gave another slow, deliberate nod. "Might be I could take a look," he said, his voice carefully neutral. "Depends on the trouble. And depends on what Walsenberg has to offer a man who's ridden a long way."

A visible wave of relief washed over the men on the steps. Jed's shoulders sagged slightly. "Thank you," he said, his voice thick with emotion. "Thank you, friend. Come on up. We'll get you something hot to drink. We can talk inside." He gestured towards the imposing doors of the courthouse.

As Tweese started towards the steps, the weight of the armored jacket felt like a costume, a useful prop. The settlers, with their hopes and fears, were simply the latest marks in a long game. Their eagerness to believe he was something more, something powerful, just made his path to fuel and a meal that much smoother. He'd play the part they'd cast for him, for as long as it suited his needs.

The interior of the courthouse was vast and cold, despite a sputtering fire in a makeshift brazier fashioned from an old oil drum in the center of what must have once been a grand foyer. The high, vaulted ceilings were lost in shadow, and the marble floors were cracked and grimy, littered with debris. The air smelled of damp stone, woodsmoke, and unwashed bodies. It was clear that this building, once a symbol of law and order, was now a beleaguered sanctuary for a community clinging to survival.

Jed led him to a rickety table near the fire, where a woman with tired eyes and work-roughened hands ladled a thin, watery stew into a chipped enamel bowl. She offered it to Tweese with a shy, hopeful smile. He took it, the warmth seeping into his chilled fingers. It wasn't much, but it was more than he'd had all day.

"This is my wife, Martha," Jed said. "And these are some of our council. Samuel, Thomas." He indicated the men who had been on the steps with him. They nodded at Tweese, their expressions still a mixture of apprehension and hope. The little boy he'd seen in the window peeked around Martha's legs, his eyes fixed on Tweese's jacket.

"So," Tweese said, after taking a few spoonfuls of the surprisingly flavorful stew. It tasted of root vegetables and some kind of stringy, unidentifiable meat. "What's this trouble you're having?"

Jed sighed, running a hand over his stubbled jaw. "It's... well, it ain't raiders, not exactly. Not the organized kind, anyway. It's the stores, see? Our food stores. Something's been getting into them. Regular as clockwork, past few months. Taking just enough to be a problem, not enough to make us starve outright, but winter's coming. We lose much more, and..." He didn't finish the sentence. He didn't need to.

"Something?" Tweese asked, raising an eyebrow. "Not someone?"

Samuel, the man who'd been holding the pipe wrench, spoke up. "We ain't sure. We set guards, but whatever it is, it's clever. Sneaky. Some say it's... it's just ruthless scavs, the kind that'll slit your throat for a mouthful of meal. Maybe holing up in them old service tunnels during the day. Others say it's just desperate folk from the shanties outside town, too cowardly to face us direct."

Tweese felt a faint tightening in his own gut. *Ruthless scavs.* He was a scavenger himself, though he preferred to think he wasn't the throat-slitting kind. Still, the description was a little too close for comfort. If these settlers were already spooked by scavengers, they wouldn't take kindly to discovering one in their midst, wearing a stolen jacket.

"And you want me to... what? Hunt down some scavs? Catch a thief?" Tweese kept his tone skeptical, pushing past the flicker of unease. This sounded like a local squabble, a problem born of their own inefficiency or lack of resolve. The kind of thing a functioning community should be able to handle themselves. *Perfect,* he thought. *Low risk, high reward.*

"We need someone who knows how to handle... situations," Jed said, choosing his words carefully. "Someone with... authority. Someone who ain't afraid. The Iron Way... you deal with worse than this every day, I reckon. Clear the roads, fight off the real monsters."

Tweese almost snorted. *If only you knew.* He was a master of bluffing his way *out* of fights, not striding into them. But their perception was his reality, at least for now. Their belief in the Iron Way mythos was his shield.

"We think it's coming from the old granary, down by the river," Thomas, the man with the rebar, added. "That place is half-collapsed, full of shadows. None of us got the stomach to go poking around in there proper, especially after dark. That's when it happens, mostly. Under cover of night."

Complacency. Neglect. Fear of the dark. Tweese recognized the symptoms. These weren't people facing an overwhelming force; these were people who had let a small problem fester, probably due to their own internal disorganization or lack of will, until it seemed insurmountable to them. He'd seen it before. They were waiting for someone to tell them what to do, or to do it for them.

And he was happy to oblige, for the right price.

"If I take a look," Tweese said slowly, drawing out the moment, "and if I solve this... problem... for you, the fuel you mentioned. How much are we talking?" He needed to keep up the appearance of a pragmatic, business-like Iron Way rider, someone who expected compensation for services rendered.

Jed's face lit up. "We can fill your tank. We've got a small stash of rendered fat-fuel, good quality. And a full pack of food for the road. Dried meat, some preserved vegetables. Best we can offer."

It was a fair trade, more than fair if the problem was as simple as he suspected. It would keep him in their good graces, keep the charade alive a little longer. Long enough to get what he needed and move on.

"Alright," Tweese said, pushing the empty stew bowl away. "Come morning, I'll take a look at your granary. But I'll need one of you to show me the way. And tell me everything you know about these... incursions."

He saw the relief, so potent it was almost palpable, wash over them. Martha even clasped her hands together as if in prayer. The little boy, emboldened, took a step closer, his eyes still fixed on the embossed knights on Tweese's jacket.

They're buying it hook, line, and sinker, Tweese thought, a flicker of grim satisfaction, not pride, touching his lips. Just a scavenger in a stolen coat, playing a role. For tonight, he had a roof, a meal, and the promise of fuel. In this world, that was a win. He'd play his part, solve their little mystery, and be on his way. What could possibly go wrong?

CHAPTER 2: THE WALSENBERG PERFORMANCE

T weese awoke to the dull ache of abused muscles and the persistent chill of the pre-dawn air, a chill that even the heavy Iron Way jacket couldn't entirely banish. He'd been given a relatively sheltered spot near the dying embers of the brazier in the courthouse foyer, a thin, scratchy blanket offered by Martha his only other comfort. It was leagues better than sleeping exposed in the ruins of Trinidad, but a cold marble floor had a way of leaching warmth from a man's bones.

He sat up, wincing as his back protested, and surveyed his surroundings in the gloom. The grand space, designed for the pronouncements of forgotten laws and the passage of important men, now felt like a mausoleum for a dead era, its remaining occupants small and fragile against its decaying majesty.

A few other settlers were stirring, their movements slow and stiff, wrapped in their own ragged coverings. Their faces, briefly illuminated by the orange glow as someone poked the embers, were etched with a familiar weariness he'd seen in countless other struggling settlements. The vast, echoing space of the foyer, with its high, shadowed ceiling and grand, crumbling staircases, dwarfed the small huddle of humanity clustered around the feeble memory of a fire. It was a stark illustration of their precarious existence: a handful of survivors clinging to a relic of a dead world, a world whose grandeur only served to highlight their own diminished state. *They're like hermit crabs in a king's discarded shell,* Tweese thought, *rattling around in something far too big for them, and probably forgetting how to build their own.*

Jed was already on his feet, speaking in low tones to Samuel near the main doors, which were now barred by a heavy timber beam – a flimsy deterrent, in Tweese's estimation, against anyone truly determined. The lantern from the previous night sat on the floor beside them, unlit. As if sensing Tweese was awake, Jed looked over and gave a curt nod, his expression unreadable in the dim light.

"Morning," Jed said, his voice still thick with sleep, though his eyes held a spark of anxious anticipation. "Hope you rested some. Martha's got some chicory boiling, if you've a taste for it. Not much else to offer for breakfast, I'm afraid. Times ain't what they were."

"Chicory's fine," Tweese replied, getting to his feet and stretching, trying to work the stiffness out of his limbs. He needed to maintain the persona – capable, perhaps a little aloof, not overly friendly. An Iron Way rider wouldn't be gushing with gratitude for a cup of bitter root-water, nor would he engage in idle chit-chat about 'better days.' "Ready to take a look at this granary of yours when you are."

A few minutes later, a tin cup of steaming, acrid chicory in hand – it tasted like burnt dirt, but it was warm – Tweese stood with Jed at the courthouse entrance. The sun was just beginning to cast a watery, grey light over Walsenberg, revealing more of its dilapidated state. Buildings leaned against each other for support, their windows like vacant eyes. Weeds grew thick in the cracked streets, nature's slow, inexorable reclamation project. There was a pervasive sense of decay, of a place slowly surrendering to the inevitable, not with a fight, but with a weary sigh.

"Thomas will take you," Jed said, nodding towards the younger man who had been part of the welcoming committee the night before, the one armed with the sharpened rebar. Thomas approached, his eyes still holding that mixture of fear and hopeful reverence, like a parishioner approaching a stern saint's relic. He seemed to have slept even less than Tweese, if the dark circles under his eyes were any indication. "He knows the granary, and what's been happening, as well as anyone. He... he used to help his father with the stores, back when his father was on the council."

"Alright, Thomas," Tweese said, fixing him with what he hoped was an assessing gaze. He needed to project competence, a hint of impatience. "Lead on. And on the way, you can tell me exactly what we're up against." He needed to hear their version of events again, gauge their level of fear, and look for inconsistencies he could exploit or use to make his eventual "solution" seem more impressive. More importantly, he needed to understand the true measure of their complacency.

As they walked, Thomas proved to be a nervous but talkative guide, his words tumbling out in a rush, as if he'd been waiting for someone, anyone, to finally listen. He clutched his rebar spear like a talisman, its sharpened point glinting dully, his head constantly swiveling, scanning rooftops and shadowed alleyways with an almost comical anxiety.

"It started a few months back, like Jed said," Thomas began, his voice hushed despite the emptiness of the street, which only amplified the sound of their footsteps. "Little things at first. A sack of grain torn open, some dried meat gone. We thought it was rats, maybe. Big ones, mind you. Or just... carelessness. Old Man Hemlock, he was on watch then, his eyes ain't what they used to be." He shook his head, a gesture of fond exasperation that quickly faded. "We… we used to have it better organized. My pa, he always said, 'A tight ship don't leak, son.' He kept things proper. The stores were tallied, the watch was regular. But since he… since he passed…"

Tweese nodded, saying nothing, letting the man talk. The familiar story: a capable hand gone, and the slow unraveling begins. It was the way of things. Structures, like bodies, decayed without constant tending.

"But it got worse," Thomas continued, his voice cracking slightly. "More regular. And always from the granary. That's where we keep the bulk of our winter stores, see? It's… it's the old co-op building, down by the river. Stone walls, mostly. Should be secure. Pa always said it was built to last, from the Before Times."

"Should be," Tweese echoed, noncommittally. He'd seen plenty of Before Times structures that hadn't lasted, precisely because the people *after* hadn't bothered to maintain them.

"We tried boarding up the broken windows, patched the holes in the roof best we could. Jed's good with his hands, but… well, there's only so much one man can do, and folks get tired, you know? Tired of patching, tired of worrying." Thomas gestured vaguely at a nearby building whose front wall was visibly bowing outwards. "Used to be, we'd have a work crew on something like that in a day. Now… now we just hope it don't fall on anyone. We even started setting a watch at the granary. But whatever's doing this… it's cunning." Thomas shivered, though the morning air was still. "They don't come when the watch is close. They know. And the… the *scavs*… Samuel's right, some of 'em are just ruthless." He glanced at Tweese, perhaps remembering his imposing presence, the jacket, the implied power. "Not like you, of course. You're… different. Orderly. Purposeful. But these others? They're like animals. Desperate."

Tweese thought of his own recent desperation, pushing the bike, his belly aching with hunger. The line between 'orderly' and 'desperate' could be a thin one, crossed in a matter of a few missed meals or a string of bad luck. He wondered if Thomas saw the irony, or if he was too caught up in the image of the Iron Way rider to see the scavenger beneath.

"They say some of 'em live in the old service tunnels that run under the town, near the river," Thomas continued, his voice dropping further, a conspiratorial edge creeping in. "Only come out at night. Quick. Quiet. Take what they need and vanish back into the dark. That's why some folks are so spooked. It ain't natural, living like that, in the dirt and the dark, like... like burrowing things. Not human things."

Tweese had to suppress a smile. It sounded less like unnatural fiends and more like canny scavengers who knew how to exploit a soft target. People living in tunnels weren't unheard of; in some of the bigger ruins, it was the only way to find shelter from the elements or the more organized gangs. But to these sheltered settlers, who clung to the crumbling edifice of a courthouse, it clearly represented something alien and terrifying. Their fear, he noted, was a useful tool. The more monstrous the perceived threat, the more heroic his eventual (and likely simple) solution would appear.

Their route took them through the decaying heart of Walsenberg. The further they moved from the courthouse, the more pronounced the neglect became. Buildings sagged, their roofs caved in, spilling their contents like the guts of disemboweled beasts. The silence of their passage was punctuated by the crunch of their boots on debris-strewn asphalt, and the nervous chatter of Thomas, who seemed to feel the need to fill every pause with more tales of woe or suspicion.

Tweese noted the lack of any real defensive perimeter around the core settlement where the courthouse stood. A few haphazard barricades of junked sedans or piled rubble blocked some side streets, but they looked more like suggestions than actual defenses – easily bypassed, poorly maintained. *These people are ripe for the picking,* he thought, a cold, professional assessment. *Not just by whatever's nipping at their granary, but by anyone with a bit of organization. They're treading water, thinking that's enough, but the current's pulling them out. This whole place is a slow-motion collapse, and they're just watching it happen.* It wasn't a comforting thought, even for an opportunist. Weakness on this scale could draw much bigger predators, and he didn't want to be around if that happened.

The granary itself was a squat, ugly stone building near the sluggish, brown river that marked the edge of town. Its slate roof was missing numerous tiles, looking like a gap-toothed grin, and several of its large loading bay doors hung crookedly on rusted hinges, groaning with every gust of wind. One entire corner of the building had partially collapsed, a jagged wound of fallen stones and splintered timbers, offering a clear view of the shadowy interior. Even from a distance, Tweese could see it was anything but secure. It looked like it had been forgotten, left to the mercy of time and entropy.

"That's it," Thomas said, gesturing with his rebar, his voice a little shaky. "We... we mostly use the main door, on the other side. Keep it barred. But... well, you can see it ain't exactly a fortress." He looked at Tweese, his expression pleading for reassurance, or perhaps absolution for their collective neglect.

Tweese walked slowly around the perimeter, his eyes scanning every detail with a practiced air. He wasn't an expert builder, but even he could spot a dozen obvious points of ingress. The collapsed corner was a gaping invitation. Several ground-floor windows, though boarded up, were done so with flimsy, rotting planks that a child could kick in. He peered at the muddy ground near the riverbank, noting a few faint, scuffed tracks leading towards the building – too indistinct to tell much, but they were there, fresh enough to suggest recent passage.

"Show me where you think they're getting in," Tweese said, his voice all business. He had to play this carefully. Too easy, and they might question why they needed him. Too difficult, and he might actually have to do some real work.

Thomas led him to a section of the wall near the collapsed corner. "We... we found some sacks dragged this way a few times. And there's a small hatch, used to be for loading grain chutes, we think. Pa showed me once. We tried piling stones against it, but..." He trailed off, shrugging helplessly, the gesture speaking volumes about their half-hearted efforts.

Tweese knelt by the hatch. It was low to the ground, made of heavy timber, but the wood was soft with rot around the edges, flaking away under his touch. The stones piled against it were a pathetic collection, easily shifted. He gave the hatch a tug; it was secured from the inside, but the frame itself felt loose, the surrounding mortar crumbling. With a little leverage, a pry bar or even a sturdy kick, it would pop right open. He could also see daylight through several gaps in the stonework nearby, where mortar had turned to dust and fallen away.

He stood up, brushing dust from his jacket, a jacket that suddenly felt like a very effective disguise. Internally, he was almost laughing. This wasn't the work of cunning, tunnel-dwelling masterminds or ruthless scavs employing sophisticated tactics. This was basic opportunism, exploiting breathtakingly poor security. A determined badger could probably get into this place. The only thing surprising was that the entire granary hadn't been emptied long ago.

But he couldn't let Thomas, or the others, know that. His payment, his precious fuel, depended on this being a significant problem that required the expertise of an Iron Way rider. "Right," Tweese said, adopting a grim expression, letting a thoughtful frown crease his brow. "This is... problematic. The whole structure's compromised." He ran a hand along a crumbling section of wall, dislodging a shower of grit. "Years of neglect. It's a miracle you haven't lost more. These things... they don't fix themselves. Leave a crack, it becomes a breach. Leave a breach, you invite the wolves."

Thomas looked even more worried, his knuckles white on his rebar spear. "Can you... can you fix it? Or stop them?"

"Stopping them is the priority," Tweese said, striding a few paces away, appearing to study the collapsed corner with intense concentration, as if deciphering ancient runes in the fallen stones. He made a show of sighting along the roofline, then squinting at the distant tree line across the river, his hand shielding his eyes like a seasoned scout. This was theater, and he was the lead actor, playing to an audience of one, who would then report back to the rest of the cast. "I need to understand their routes, their methods. This isn't just about patching a hole. This is about understanding the enemy." *The enemy being a leaky building and some half-starved opportunists taking advantage of a gift-wrapped opportunity,* he added silently.

He spent the next hour in a parody of a meticulous investigation. He had Thomas point out every spot where grain had been spilled ("See here? Drag marks. Hasty. But not panicked. They feel comfortable."), every suspected point of entry ("Too obvious. A feint, perhaps?"), every shadow that seemed too deep ("They'd use this approach. The dead ground favors them."). He climbed onto a section of relatively stable low roof and "scouted" the surroundings, his gaze lingering on nothing in particular but delivered with an air of profound strategic assessment. He made vague, serious-sounding pronouncements. "The river provides cover... they're using the blind spots... a pattern is emerging... they are bolder than I thought." It was all nonsense, of course, designed to build suspense and justify his presence, but Thomas seemed to hang on his every word, his initial fear now mixed with a palpable sense of relief that someone, finally, was *doing something*, someone who seemed to know what they were about.

Tweese knew what the real problem was: a combination of decay, shoddy repair work, and a complete lack of systematic security. The "raids" were likely the work of a few individuals, or perhaps even just one or two, who had discovered how laughably easy it was to pilfer from the granary. They probably weren't even part of an organized group, just locals or passing scavs who'd stumbled upon an easy meal ticket and couldn't believe their luck. The fact that the settlers hadn't caught them yet spoke volumes about their vigilance, or lack thereof.

His "solution" would have to be two-fold. First, he'd need to recommend some actual, practical repairs – things that would make the granary marginally more secure, enough to satisfy the settlers and perhaps deter the most casual thief. Simple things, really: better barricades, patching the more obvious holes, maybe even a tripwire or two if he felt ambitious. Second, and more importantly for his performance, he'd need to do something dramatic, something that *looked* like he was confronting a dangerous threat. Something that would justify his reward and solidify his reputation as a capable Iron Way enforcer.

"Alright," he said finally, hopping down from a low wall, a look of dawning realization on his face, as if a complex puzzle had just snapped into place. "I think I see what's happening here. It's not as simple as a few holes in the wall." He paused for effect, letting his gaze sweep over the dilapidated granary. "They're being systematic. Coordinated." He let that sink in, watching Thomas's eyes widen with fresh alarm. "But they've made mistakes. They've left signs, subtle, but there for a trained eye." He tapped the side of his nose. "And tonight," he declared, with a steely glint in his eye he hoped looked convincing, "we're going to use those mistakes against them." He had no concrete plan yet for the "tonight" part, but he knew it needed to be something more than just showing them how to stack rocks properly or patch a hole with scavenged planks. He needed a flourish, a bit of excitement to seal the deal. The fuel, the food, his safe passage – it all depended on a good show. And Phillip Tweese, if nothing else, knew how to put on a show.

The rest of the morning and a good part of the afternoon were dedicated to Tweese's elaborate, and largely performative, preparations. He knew the settlers, particularly Jed, Samuel, and the ever-anxious Thomas, were watching his every move, their faces a mixture of hope and trepidation. He had to make this look good. A simple, practical solution wouldn't have the same impact, wouldn't justify the Iron Way mystique he was so carefully cultivating. This wasn't just about scaring off a few petty thieves; it was about cementing his role, ensuring his payment, and getting out of Walsenberg with a full tank and a story they'd tell for weeks – a story that would, hopefully, keep other, more dangerous scavs at bay long after he was gone.

"Alright," Tweese announced, after another cup of Martha's chicory – which seemed to get more bitter with each cup – and a meager ration of dry, crumbly bread that did little to appease the gnawing in his stomach. He addressed Jed and Samuel, who had gathered with Thomas in the courthouse foyer, a makeshift command center that smelled faintly of dust and desperation. Martha hovered nearby, her hands clasped, her expression one of weary hope. "The situation at the granary is, as I said, a result of systematic exploitation of your vulnerabilities." He used the word "vulnerabilities" deliberately; it sounded more professional, more serious, than just saying 'your building's falling apart and your security is a joke.' It also subtly shifted the blame from their inaction to some external, cunning force.

"These scavs," he continued, pacing a short line before them, his hands clasped behind his back in what he hoped was a thoughtful, authoritative pose – a trick he'd learned from watching a traveling preacher con a village out of their winter supplies years ago. "They're not fools. They know your routines. They know your weaknesses. They've been testing you, pushing the boundaries, seeing how much they can get away with." He saw Jed and Samuel exchange a grim look. Good. Let them think this was a calculated campaign against them, not just opportunistic pilfering by a few hungry individuals. Fear made people compliant. Fear made them grateful for saviors.

"So, tonight, we turn the tables." Tweese stopped pacing and met their eyes, letting his gaze linger on each of them for a moment. "We won't just be waiting for them. We'll be setting a trap. Something they won't expect."

"A trap?" Thomas breathed, his eyes wide, his grip tightening on the rebar spear he now carried everywhere. "Like... with snares? Or... or pits dug in the ground?"

Tweese almost smiled. The boy's imagination was running wild, probably fueled by old stories or exaggerated tales of wasteland justice. "Something a little more... definitive, Thomas. We need to send a message. Not just to these particular thieves, but to any others who might be watching, thinking Walsenberg is an easy mark." He let that sink in. The idea of sending a broader message, of re-establishing some kind of deterrence, would appeal to their beleaguered pride and their deep-seated fear of the outside world.

His actual plan was far less dramatic, and certainly less lethal, than his pronouncements suggested. The core of it was simple: make a lot of noise, create some confusion, and ensure that whatever (or whoever) was raiding the granary was scared off, preferably without any actual confrontation that might put *him* at risk. The key was the performance, the illusion of overwhelming force and preparedness.

"First," he said, turning to Jed, "we need to make the granary *look* less inviting, but not so secure that our friends decide to try a different, more difficult approach tonight. We want them to come to the usual spot." He was thinking of the rotten hatch Thomas had shown him. It was the most likely point of entry for a casual thief, the path of least resistance. "We'll reinforce some of the more obvious breaches – those broken windows, the collapsed corner. Just enough to make it seem like you've made an effort. But we leave their preferred route… accessible."

Jed frowned, his brow furrowing. "Leave it open? But… isn't that what we're trying to stop? Seems like inviting the fox into the henhouse."

"It's called channeling, Jed," Tweese said, improvising with a term he thought sounded suitably tactical, something a seasoned Iron Way commander might say. "We want them to think they're still in control, that they've found a way around your new, flimsy defenses. We draw them into a kill-zone." He conveniently omitted the fact that he had no intention of actually 'killing' anyone, nor did he believe these particular scavs warranted such a response. His primary concern was his own skin, and then his payment.

Over the next few hours, Tweese directed a small, reluctant work crew, consisting mostly of Thomas and a couple of other younger, skittish men whose names he hadn't bothered to learn, in the "fortification" of the granary. He had them drag heavy timbers – salvaged from other collapsed buildings, their wood grey and splintered – and wedge them against the inside of the worst of the broken windows. He instructed them to pile more stones, larger ones this time, around the base of the collapsed corner, making it look more difficult to scramble through, though a determined individual with a bit of agility could still manage it. It was all for show, busywork to make the settlers feel like they were participating in a serious defensive operation, to give them a sense of agency they clearly lacked. He watched them struggle, their movements often clumsy, their efforts lacking the efficiency of desperation he'dseen in true survivors. These were people who had forgotten how to truly fight for what was theirs, or perhaps had never learned.

He paid particular attention to the area around the rotten hatch. "This is where they'll likely try," he told Thomas, pointing with a decisive finger. "It's concealed, it's low. Classic infiltrator's route. They'll see the other work you've done, assume you've overlooked this spot, or that you're not thorough." He had them clear some of the debris from around it, making the approach slightly easier, but subtly ensured that the hatch itself remained the path of least resistance. He even had one of the younger men scrape away some of the more obvious cobwebs, muttering something about "not wanting to give them any warning."

While the others worked, grunting and sweating with the unaccustomed labor under the weak afternoon sun, Tweese himself did a lot of pointing, striding, and thoughtful chin-stroking. He'd occasionally pick up a rock, examine it with great seriousness as if divining its strategic properties, then instruct one of the settlers to place it in a slightly different position, perhaps a few inches to the left. He made a show of checking sightlines from various points inside the granary, of pacing out distances between potential cover and the "kill-zone," muttering to himself about fields of fire and ambush points. He knew he was laying it on thick, but the settlers seemed to be eating it up. They were desperate for leadership, for someone to tell them that their problems were solvable, even if the solutions were dramatic and a little terrifying. Their gratitude, their almost childlike faith in his pronouncements, was a strange and, if he were honest, slightly unsettling sensation. He wasn't used to it. He was used to suspicion, to wary negotiation, to the quick calculations of the street. This open-faced trust felt… odd.

"Now, for the… reception committee," Tweese said, once the superficial repairs were done to his satisfaction. He gathered Jed, Samuel, and Thomas near the main door of the granary, the air inside cool and musty. "Tonight, when our visitors arrive, we need to make it clear they've made a mistake. A big one."

His "trap" was laughably simple, relying more on psychological impact than actual danger. He'd found several large, empty metal drums in a shed behind the courthouse, probably once used for storing water or fuel. He also located a few lengths of rusted chain and some loose sheets of corrugated iron that had once been roofing, their edges jagged and sharp. Perfect noisemakers.

"We'll position ourselves inside, near the hatch," he explained, drawing a crude map in the dust on the granary floor with the toe of his boot. "When they make their move, when they're committed – halfway through the hatch, perhaps, or when the first one is fully inside – that's when we make our presence known. Loudly." He gestured to the drums and chains. "Noise. Confusion. The element of surprise. Most scavs, the kind you're dealing with, they're cowards at heart. They prey on the weak, the unprepared. A sudden, aggressive response, the sound of a superior force, they'll scatter like rats."

"So... we just scare them off?" Samuel asked, a hint of disappointment in his voice. He was a burly man, his hands calloused, and Tweese suspected he'd been hoping for a more... final solution, perhaps a chance to use that heavy pipe wrench for something other than tightening bolts.

Tweese fixed him with a hard look, the kind he imagined an Iron Way enforcer might use. "Scare them off *this time*, Samuel. And make them think twice about ever coming back. An Iron Way rider doesn't need to spill blood to make a point, not always. Sometimes, a clear demonstration of capability, of *readiness*, is enough. They'll spread the word: Walsenberg is no longer a soft touch. The Iron Way has an interest here." He hoped that last part sounded suitably ominous and protective. It seemed to satisfy Samuel, who nodded slowly, though his grip on the pipe wrench didn't loosen.

The real genius of the plan, from Tweese's perspective, was that it required very little from him in terms of actual risk. He'd be there, of course, to "lead" the response, to give the signal. But the settlers would be the ones making most of the noise, and if, by some mischance, the scavs decided to fight back – which he highly doubted, given their previous timidity – well, Jed and Samuel had their own weapons. He had his .45, but he had no intention of using that precious single armor-piercing round on some petty thief unless his own skin was directly on the line. That bullet was for a much bigger problem, if one arose.

As dusk began to settle, casting long, distorted shadows across the decaying town and painting the sky in hues of bruised purple and fading orange, Tweese led his small party back to the granary. He had them carry the metal drums, the chains, and the sheets of iron inside, placing them strategically in the dusty, cavernous interior, not far from the rotten hatch, as per his "map." The place smelled of mildew, old grain, and rodent droppings – a familiar scent from countless other abandoned buildings he'd explored. Shafts of fading light pierced the gloom through holes in the roof, illuminating dancing dust motes like tiny, indifferent stars.

"Alright," Tweese said, his voice a low command in the echoing space, trying to project an authority he didn't entirely feel but knew was essential for the role. "Jed, you and Samuel take positions here, behind these sacks." He indicated a pile of what looked like empty grain bags, offering some minimal cover and a good angle on the hatch. "When I give the signal – and *only* when I give the signal, understand? No heroics, no jumping the gun – you start hitting those drums with whatever you've got. Chains, rebar, make it sound like a damned foundry exploding. I want them to think the sky is falling in on them."

Jed nodded, his face grim. Samuel hefted his pipe wrench with a certain grim satisfaction.

"Thomas, you'll be with me, by the hatch. You'll have one of these." He handed Thomas a sheet of corrugated iron. "When the time comes, you bang this against the stone wall. Hard. As loud as you can. Got it?"

Thomas, looking pale but resolute in the dimming light, nodded, gripping the iron sheet tightly, his knuckles white. He looked like a boy about to face his first real monster, and Tweese felt a fleeting, almost uncomfortable pang of something that might have been pity, or perhaps just a detached professional interest in how his actors would perform.

"And what will *you* be doing?" Jed asked, his eyes narrowed slightly. It was the first sign of anything less than complete trust Tweese had seen from him, a slight crack in the facade of the grateful settler. He was probably wondering if the "Iron Way rider" was going to put himself in the line of fire.

Tweese met his gaze coolly, unflinchingly. "I'll be the one to greet our guests. And I'll be the one to decide when the party starts." He patted the .45 holstered under his jacket, a subtle reminder of his own (supposed) capability and the authority he was projecting. "Don't worry, Jed. I know what I'm doing." He hoped he sounded more confident than he felt. This whole charade was a gamble, and the stakes were higher than just a tank of fuel. If this went wrong, if the "scavs" were more numerous or more determined than he anticipated, or if the settlers lost their nerve and fumbled their parts...

He pushed the thought aside. He was a con man, and this was his stage. He'd set the scene, directed his actors. Now all that was left was to wait for the curtain to rise on the night's performance. He found a relatively concealed spot in the deep shadows near the hatch, a spot that offered a quick retreat through a different, less obvious hole in the wall if necessary. He settled down to wait, the granary's deep silence disturbed by the nervous, shallow breathing of Thomas beside him and the distant, mournful cry of some night bird. The smell of dust and decay was thick in his nostrils. It was going to be a long night.

The hours in the granary crawled by with agonizing slowness, each tick of an imaginary clock amplified in the oppressive stillness.

The last vestiges of twilight bled from the sky, leaving the cavernous interior steeped in a profound, unnerving blackness, pierced only by the faint, ghostly luminescence of the moon filtering through the holes in the roof. These pale shafts of light painted shifting, ethereal patterns on the dusty floor and the stacked sacks of grain, transforming familiar shapes into monstrous, lurking figures. Every creak of the old building settling under the night's chill, every rustle of unseen vermin skittering within the ancient stone walls, every gust of wind that moaned through the broken windows like a dying breath, stretched Tweese's nerves tighter. He wasn't afraid of the dark, or of whatever petty thieves might be foolish enough to try their luck. He'd spent a good portion of his life navigating far more dangerous shadows. No, he was afraid of the unknown variables, the things his carefully constructed con couldn't account for – a more determined band of scavs, a settler losing their nerve at the critical moment, an unexpected patrol from some other, less predictable gang.

Beside him, Thomas was a bundle of barely suppressed jitters. Tweese could hear the young man's shallow, rapid breathing, the occasional nervous swallow that sounded unnaturally loud in the quiet. The sheet of corrugated iron Thomas clutched vibrated faintly with his tremors, creating a tiny, almost inaudible metallic whisper. *Kid's going to drop it or start screaming before anything even happens,* Tweese thought with a flash of irritation. He needed Thomas to hold it together, at least for a little while. A panicked participant could unravel the whole performance.

"Easy, Thomas," Tweese murmured, his voice a low rumble that barely carried over the sighing of the wind. He kept his tone even, projecting a calm he didn't entirely feel. "Deep breaths. Remember what I told you. We're ready for them. They're the ones walking into *our* house tonight, not the other way around." He hoped the feigned confidence was contagious, or at least enough to settle the boy's most immediate fears. He'd seen raw fear cripple tougher men than Thomas.

Across the dusty expanse, hidden behind their barricade of empty sacks, Jed and Samuel were equally still, equally tense. Tweese could just make out their silhouettes against the slightly less opaque darkness of a distant, boarded-up window. He trusted them to follow his instructions, if only because their fear of the alternative – facing the "scavs" alone and unprepared, as they had been doing for months – was likely greater than their fear of his plan. Jed, at least, had a shotgun, though Tweese suspected he was more accustomed to threatening with it than actually firing it in anger. Samuel's pipe wrench looked more like a tool of desperation than a practiced weapon. Still, their presence, their willingness to participate, was crucial to the illusion of strength.

Time stretched and warped, the way it always did during a long, tense wait. Tweese found himself drifting, his mind replaying the events of the past two days: the incredible, almost unbelievable luck of finding the bike, the crushing disappointment of running out of fuel so quickly, the unexpected turn of events here in Walsenberg. It was a strange, almost surreal situation. He, Phillip Tweese, a man whose survival depended on a sharp eye and quick wits, was now an "Iron Way rider," a supposed bastion of order and strength, about to lead a band of frightened settlers against... well, against what, exactly? He still suspected it was nothing more than a few desperate souls, maybe even kids, driven by hunger. But he'd built it up in their minds, painted a picture of cunning, coordinated thieves, and now he had to deliver a performance worthy of the billing. The irony wasn't lost on him. He was manipulating them into feeling secure by making them believe they were in greater danger than they probably were.

He thought about past tight spots, the countless times he'd had to think fast to keep his belly full and a roof, any roof, over his head, especially during his drift north from the harsh, sun-baked lands to the south. He'd learned early that a quick mind and a plausible story often went further than a strong arm, especially when resources were thin and everyone was wary. Sometimes it was a carefully spun tale that opened a door or earned a meal, other times a bit of opportune scavenging when no one was looking, or just knowing when to talk fast and when to disappear before questions got too pointed. The goal was always the same: get what he needed to see the next sunrise, to keep moving, to stay one step ahead of whatever hardship was snapping at his heels. This situation in Walsenberg, though, this was different. The stakes felt... fuzzier. He wasn't just after a meal or a few trinkets. He was after fuel, a significant prize. But he was also, inadvertently, dealing in hope, a commodity he usually avoided as it tended to complicate things, made people clingy, made departures messy.

A faint scraping sound from outside, near the rotten hatch, snapped him back to full alertness. His senses, honed by years of needing to detect the slightest hint of danger or opportunity, zeroed in on the noise. Thomas stiffened beside him, letting out a tiny, involuntary gasp that was quickly stifled. Tweese put a warning hand on the young man's arm, a firm, steady pressure. *Showtime.*

The scraping came again, louder this time, more deliberate, followed by a muffled thud, as if something heavy – a sack, perhaps, for carrying away loot – had been set down. Then, the distinct, cautious creak of wood yielding to pressure. Tweese could almost visualize it: someone prying at the rotten frame of the hatch, testing its give, their movements economical, practiced. His own heart began to beat a little faster, not with fear, but with the familiar adrenaline surge of a con about to reach its critical moment, the point where the bluff either held or spectacularly collapsed.

He waited, straining his ears, every nerve ending alive. A low murmur of voices, too indistinct to make out words, but clearly more than one person. Then another creak, more sustained this time, followed by a soft splintering sound. The hatch was opening. He could hear the faint scuffing of boots on the packed earth outside, then on the stone sill of the hatch itself. One shadow, then another, resolved itself in the narrow opening, darker shapes against the lesser dark of the night. They were moving slowly, cautiously, as he'd expected, like animals testing the air before entering a new den. He counted two, maybe three figures, hunched low.

He let the first figure get halfway through the hatch, a hunched silhouette, its head turning this way and that, trying to pierce the interior gloom. He needed them committed, at least one of them inside, off-balance. He didn't reach for his .45. That was for a real threat, for a life-or-death situation. This called for theater, for overwhelming, disorienting shock.

"*Now!*" Tweese roared, his voice, amplified by the echoing acoustics of the granary, sounding like the crack of doom, a sudden, savage explosion of sound in the tomblike silence.

The effect was instantaneous and immensely satisfying. The figure in the hatch yelped, a high-pitched sound of pure terror, and scrambled backward with comical haste, legs flailing, thudding heavily into whatever or whoever was directly behind him. Simultaneously, on Tweese's command, Jed and Samuel erupted into a cacophony of noise. The metal drums boomed like cannons as they were struck with rebar and lengths of chain with a desperate fury. The chains themselves were rattled and smashed against the stone floor, creating a hellish, clanging din that seemed to shake the very foundations of the old building. Thomas, after a frozen second of panic where his eyes went wide as dinner plates, remembered his part and began to hammer the corrugated iron sheet against the granary wall with all his might, the metallic shrieks adding to the pandemonium, a high, tearing counterpoint to the booming drums.

It sounded, Tweese thought with grim satisfaction, like a small army was dismantling the building from the inside out, or perhaps like a very angry, very large metal beast had been awakened from a long slumber and was now expressing its displeasure.

He himself added to the effect, letting out another guttural roar – a sound he'd practiced in his more solitary scavenging days to scare off feral dogs – and kicking over a stack of loose planks he'd noticed earlier, sending them clattering across the floor with a satisfying crash. He stayed in the shadows, making no move to expose himself. The illusion of a powerful, unseen, and numerous force was far more effective than revealing himself as a single man orchestrating the chaos. Let their imaginations fill in the terrifying details.

Outside the hatch, there were shouts of alarm, panicked curses, and the distinct sound of feet stumbling and fleeing in multiple directions. Tweese could hear them crashing through the underbrush near the riverbank, their retreat anything but stealthy, the sounds of their flight punctuated by more yelps and what sounded like someone tripping and falling heavily. It was over in less than thirty seconds. The sudden, overwhelming, and utterly unexpected wave of sheer noise had done its job perfectly. No finesse, no subtlety, just raw, auditory shock and awe.

He let his own men continue their racket for another half-minute, just to be sure, to give the intruders ample time to put as much distance as possible between themselves and this suddenly very unwelcoming granary. Then, he raised a hand, though it was too dark for them to see it clearly. "Alright! Hold it! Hold it!" he bellowed, his voice cutting through their enthusiastic noise-making.

Gradually, the din subsided, replaced by the ringing in Tweese's ears and the heavy, panting breaths of Jed, Samuel, and a visibly shaking Thomas. The silence that followed felt immense, charged, almost electric with the lingering adrenaline.

"They're gone," Tweese announced, his voice calm and authoritative, though his own heart was still thumping from the manufactured excitement. He stepped out of the shadows, peering cautiously towards the hatch. Nothing. Just the cold night air, the distant croaking of frogs from the river, and the lingering smell of fear – or perhaps that was just the ever-present mildew. "Didn't even wait to see who was throwing the party."

Jed and Samuel emerged from behind their barricade, their faces flushed in the dim moonlight, eyes bright with a mixture of adrenaline and dawning relief. Samuel was grinning, hefting his pipe wrench like a trophy. "That was… that was something!" Jed exclaimed, shaking his head in disbelief, a wide grin spreading across his face. "Never heard a noise like it! Sounded like the sky was caving in! You think they'll be back?"

"Not tonight," Tweese said confidently, though he made a mental note to suggest they properly secure the hatch in the morning. "And maybe not ever, if they've got any sense. They came expecting sheep, and they found… well, they found something else." He let them fill in the blank. *The Iron Way.* Let the legend do the heavy lifting.

Thomas was leaning against the wall, the iron sheet clattered at his feet, his face pale but with a dazed, almost euphoric smile playing on his lips. "I… I hit it as hard as I could," he stammered, his voice still shaky. "Did you hear it? I think I bent the metal!"

"Heard it all the way to Cheyenne, Thomas," Tweese said, clapping the young man on the shoulder with a magnanimity he didn't entirely feel but knew the role required. The kid looked like he was about to either throw up or burst into tears of relief. "You did good. You all did good. Stood your ground."

They spent another few minutes in the granary, Jed and Samuel reliving the brief, chaotic "battle," their initial fear transforming into a boisterous, exaggerated bravado. Each telling made the sounds louder, the scavs' panic more pronounced, their own bravery more steadfast. Tweese listened, nodding sagely, occasionally interjecting a comment about the "scavs' predictable cowardice when faced with unified resistance" or the "effectiveness of a decisive show of force." He made sure to reinforce the idea that this was a calculated tactical victory, a planned operation, not just a lucky scare. The narrative was important.

Finally, Jed clapped him on the back, his hand heavy and enthusiastic. "Well, Rider, I don't know how to thank you. You did what you said you would. More, even. We... we ain't felt this safe in months. Just knowing someone like you is willing to stand with us..."

"Just doing my part, Jed," Tweese said, adopting a modest but firm tone. "The roads need to be safe. Settlements need to be secure. That's the Way." He was getting good at this, spouting platitudes that sounded profound but meant very little. It was like learning lines for a play, and this audience was particularly receptive.

They made their way back to the courthouse, the mood considerably lighter than it had been on their journey to the granary. The air felt cleaner, the shadows less menacing. Word of the "victory" seemed to spread quickly, a ripple of excitement passing through the sleeping courthouse. As they entered the foyer, Martha rushed forward, her tired face alight with a gratitude that was almost painful to witness. Other settlers emerged from the shadows, their expressions hopeful, some even offering quiet words of thanks, shy smiles, as Tweese passed.

The little boy he'd seen earlier, whose name he learned was Pip, son of Jed and Martha, stared at him with undisguised hero-worship, his small hand clutching a crudely carved wooden toy that just might have been a motorcycle. He didn't say anything, just looked, his eyes reflecting the flickering light of the now-revived brazier.

It was... an unfamiliar feeling. This open gratitude, this admiration. Tweese was used to wary glances, to grudging respect earned through quick wits or a veiled threat, to the fleeting satisfaction of a successful con where the mark was left poorer but none the wiser, and he was long gone before they figured it out. This was different. These people weren't just impressed; they were genuinely, profoundly thankful. They looked at him as if he'd single-handedly slain a dragon, not just orchestrated a noisy charade to scare off a few hungry opportunists.

He found it vaguely discomfiting. Their belief in him, in the persona he'd adopted, was so absolute, so untainted by cynicism. It made the stolen jacket feel a little tighter across his shoulders, the .45 holstered beneath his jacket a little heavier, a weight of expectation he hadn't bargained for.

Later, after sharing another meager meal – though this one felt almost celebratory, the stew tasted richer, the bread less stale, or perhaps it was just the atmosphere of shared relief – Jed approached him, a look of sincere, almost boyish appreciation on his face.

"The fuel, Rider. Like we promised." He held out a heavy, sloshing canister, its sides slick with grease. It looked like an old military jerry can, battered but serviceable. "Best fat-fuel we got. Filtered it twice. Should get you a good ways north. And Martha's packed you some provisions. Dried elk, some parched corn, even a few apples we were saving for a special occasion. Reckon this qualifies."

Tweese took the canister, testing its weight. It felt substantial. This, at least, was real. Tangible. The reward for a night's work, however deceptive that work might have been. "Appreciate it, Jed," he said, his voice gruff, trying to sound like a man to whom such rewards were commonplace.

"No, friend. We appreciate *you*," Jed insisted, his voice earnest. "You gave us back a bit of hope tonight. Showed us we don't just have to... to take it. That we can fight back, if we stand together. Maybe... maybe we'd forgotten that." He paused, then added, a little awkwardly, "If... if you're ever passing this way again... Walsenberg would be honored to offer you hospitality. Proper hospitality, next time."

Tweese merely nodded, avoiding Jed's gaze. He had no intention of ever passing this way again if he could help it. His business here was concluded. He had his fuel, his food. It was time to move on, before his luck ran out, before someone saw through the cracks in his performance, or before their gratitude became too much of a burden.

Yet, as he prepared to leave in the pre-dawn gloom of the next morning, the air cold and sharp in his lungs, strapping the fuel canister and the provisions to the back of the magnificent motorcycle – *his* motorcycle, he was definitely starting to think of it that way – he found himself glancing back at the silent, hulking form of the courthouse. He saw a flicker of light in an upper window – young Pip, perhaps, already awake, looking out for the departing "hero."

For a moment, a strange, unbidden thought crossed his mind, as unwelcome and persistent as a biting fly: *It wasn't so bad, playing the good guy.* He quickly, almost violently, dismissed it. Sentimentality was a weakness, a luxury a man like him couldn't afford. He was a scavenger, an opportunist, a drifter who did what was necessary. That's who he was. The gratitude of Walsenberg, the wide eyes of a child – they were just pleasant, and profitable, side effects of a well-executed plan. Nothing more.

He swung his leg over the bike, the leather of the seat cool beneath him. The engine caught with its familiar, muted thrum, a sound that was quickly becoming his favorite in the world.

He was fueled, supplied, and pointed north. Towards Cheyenne. Towards the real Iron Way. Towards whatever came next. He didn't look back as he rode out of Walsenberg, the sound of his engine a quiet whisper in the sleeping town. He had a long road ahead, and the performance, he suspected, was far from over.

CHAPTER 3: FORGING THE RIDER

The pre-dawn air was sharp and clean in Tweese's lungs as he guided the motorcycle out of the sleeping, shadowed streets of Walsenberg. The thrum of the diesel engine, though muted, felt like a powerful heartbeat beneath him, a reassuring pulse of potential. He had a full tank of fuel, a pack laden with provisions, and the memory of young Pip's awestruck face as a peculiar, almost uncomfortable warmth in his chest – a warmth he quickly tried to extinguish with a healthy dose of pragmatism. Gratitude was fine, but fuel was better. Hope was a nice sentiment, but dried elk would get him further.

He didn't look back. Walsenberg and its problems were behind him. Ahead lay the I-25, the long, broken ribbon of asphalt leading north to Cheyenne, and, he hoped, to a new life courtesy of the Iron Way. The bike handled beautifully on the relatively open stretches of the old interstate, its weight feeling solid and planted, the custom suspension soaking up the worst of the cracks and frost heaves in the ancient concrete. For the first time in a long while, Phillip Tweese felt something akin to optimism, a dangerous but intoxicating sensation. He was a man with a powerful machine, a full belly, and a destination. It was more than most people in this decaying world could claim.

The landscape unrolled before him, a monotonous panorama of browns and greys under a vast, pale sky. Ruined farmsteads, their timbers bleached and collapsing, dotted the plains like forgotten bones. Skeletal remains of old-world vehicles lay rusting in ditches, picked clean of anything useful long ago. Occasionally, he'd see a faded, hand-painted sign by the roadside, similar to the one outside Walsenberg, proclaiming "THE LORD IS MY SHEPHERD" or "REPENT, THE END IS NIGH," their messages of faith or warning rendered almost absurd by the sheer, desolate emptiness that surrounded them. Tweese snorted. If the Lord was providing for anyone out here, He was doing it with a very light hand.

He rode for several hours, the sun climbing higher, the initial chill burning off. The fuel Jed had given him seemed to be of decent quality; the engine maintained its steady, quiet rhythm. He was making good time. His plan was to find a defensible spot to lie low during the hottest part of the day, then continue riding into the evening. The less time he spent exposed on the open road during daylight, the better.

It was mid-morning when he rounded a long, sweeping bend and saw trouble ahead. Not the kind with flashing lights or barricades, but the slow, simmering kind that often festered in isolated pockets of humanity. Two dilapidated farmsteads faced each other across a narrow, muddy gash in the earth that might have once been a creek or an irrigation channel. Further back, he could see a slightly wider, equally sluggish stream from which this channel probably originated. Between the two farmsteads, perhaps a hundred yards apart, two groups of people were engaged in a vocal, if not yet overtly violent, confrontation.

Tweese slowed the bike, pulling off to the side of the cracked road, partially concealing the motorcycle behind a clump of overgrown, thorny bushes. He cut the engine, and the sudden silence pressed in, quickly filled by the angry shouts carrying on the wind. He unslung the ancient, battered binoculars he'd salvaged years ago – serviceable enough for his needs – and focused on the scene.

There were three men on one side, armed with pitchforks and what looked like a heavy, rust-pitted wrench. On the other, two men and a woman, the men holding sharpened staves, the woman brandishing a rusty sickle with surprising ferocity. They were all shouting, gesticulating wildly. It looked like a classic land or resource dispute, the kind that could easily escalate from harsh words to spilled blood when desperation was high and a mediating authority was absent.

Just keep riding, a sensible part of his brain advised. *Not your circus, not your monkeys.* He had fuel, he had food. Getting involved was an unnecessary risk. But another part of him, the part that had successfully navigated Walsenberg by playing a role, was curious. And the jacket felt heavy on his shoulders, a silent prompt. These people looked poor, their farms on the verge of collapse. They might have little to offer in terms of trade, but the situation presented an opportunity. An opportunity to further test his newfound persona, perhaps. Or maybe, just maybe, the brief, uncomfortable warmth he'd felt from Pip's admiring gaze hadn't entirely faded. He dismissed that thought as quickly as it arose. It was about advantage, nothing more. If he could project the authority of the Iron Way here, solve their little spat, it would only solidify the legend he was unintentionally building around himself. And who knew? They might have a spare bit of jerky, or some information about the road ahead.

He remounted the bike, the quiet thrum of the engine announcing his approach as he rode slowly towards the feuding parties. As he drew closer, the shouting died down, replaced by wary, hostile stares. He saw their eyes flick to the bike, then to his jacket, the one with the knights and roses. He saw the subtle shift in their posture, the way their grip on their makeshift weapons tightened, then, almost imperceptibly, loosened. The

Iron Way reputation, it seemed, traveled far, even to these forgotten backwaters.

He brought the bike to a halt between the two groups, the engine idling with its low, rhythmic beat. He didn't dismount immediately, letting them take him in, the imposing machine, the armored rider. He pushed his goggles up onto his forehead and surveyed them coolly, his expression unreadable. "What's the trouble here?" he asked, his voice intentionally calm but carrying an edge of command.

The taller of the three men, a gaunt fellow with a stringy beard and eyes that burned with a feverish resentment, stepped forward. "This ain't your concern, Rider. This is a private matter between neighbors."

"Anything that disrupts the peace along these roads is my concern," Tweese replied, his voice flat. He was improvising, but the words felt surprisingly natural, as if he'd said them before. "Spill it. Or I'll assume you're all just common brigands squabbling over scraps, and deal with you accordingly." He let his hand rest near the .45 holstered beneath his jacket.

The threat, though vague, had its intended effect. The man's bluster deflated slightly. On the other side, the woman with the sickle spoke up, her voice sharp with anger. "They're stealing our water, Rider! That's the trouble! The Greersons here, they've dammed the ditch, taking every last drop from the Trinity fork for their own dying crops, leaving ours to wither!"

"Liar!" the gaunt man – Greerson, presumably – spat back. "The ditch runs dry because *you* lot over at the Hendersons' place let your end silt up! We ain't seen a decent flow in weeks because of your laziness!"

So it was a water dispute. As old as farming itself. Tweese looked at the muddy, nearly stagnant channel between them. It was choked with weeds and what looked like a buildup of mud and debris. He then glanced towards the main stream from which it supposedly drew water. Even from this distance, that too looked sluggish and overgrown.

"Show me this ditch," Tweese said, his gaze sweeping over both groups. "And the intake from the... Trinity fork, you called it?"

Reluctantly, but clearly intimidated by his presence and the implied authority of his jacket, the two groups led him towards the head of the irrigation ditch, a few hundred yards upstream. They walked in sullen silence, keeping a wary distance from each other, with Tweese on the motorcycle riding slowly between them like some post-apocalyptic judge.

The problem, when they reached the intake, was so glaringly obvious that Tweese almost laughed out loud. The small diversion channel leading from the Trinity fork – itself a pathetic trickle of murky water – was almost completely blocked by a fallen, half-rotted cottonwood tree, its branches and a summer's worth of accumulated leaves and debris forming a near-perfect dam. What little water managed to seep through was then further impeded by a thick layer of silt and overgrown reeds that choked the first fifty yards of the ditch itself.

It wasn't malice, or theft, or even complex engineering that was causing their water shortage. It was simple, unadulterated neglect. A problem that a few hours of hard work with shovels and axes could have easily solved weeks, if not months, ago.

Tweese looked from the clogged ditch to the angry, accusing faces of the farmers. Their resentment towards each other was so thick it was almost palpable, yet they had apparently been so consumed by their feud that neither side had bothered to walk a few hundred yards to diagnose the actual cause of their shared misery. Or, if they had, they'd each been waiting for the other to fix it.

"This," Tweese said, gesturing with a leather-gloved hand towards the fallen tree and the silted-up channel, "is your problem. Not him." He pointed at Greerson. "Nor her." He pointed at Henderson. "It's this. Neglect. Plain and simple."

The farmers stared at the blockage as if seeing it for the first time, though Tweese suspected they'd all known, on some level, what the issue was. It was easier to blame a neighbor than to organize a communal effort. "Well, I..." Greerson began, then trailed off, looking flustered. Mrs. Henderson opened her mouth, then closed it again, her face flushing slightly under its layer of grime.

"The Iron Way expects communities to manage their own resources," Tweese declared, his voice taking on a stern, almost paternal tone. He was finding this role surprisingly easy to slip into. It was like the jacket itself carried a certain weight, a certain authority. "Water is life. Squabbling over a trickle when the source is choked is... inefficient. Wasteful." He paused, letting his words hang in the air. "This blockage benefits no one. It harms you both."

He looked at the fallen tree. It was substantial, but not immovable. "You have axes? Shovels?" Both groups nodded mutely. "Then you'll clear this. Both of you. Together." He wasn't asking; he was telling. "The Hendersons will start on this side of the tree, the Greersons on the other. You'll clear the branches, then work together to shift the trunk. Then you'll both work your way down the ditch, clearing the silt and reeds until the water flows freely to both your properties. Understood?"

There was a moment of stunned silence. Then, young Thomas Henderson, who had been quiet up until now, spoke up timidly, "But... who makes sure it's... fair? That one side don't take more after?"

Tweese fixed him with a look. "You make it fair. You'll talk. You'll agree. Or, if you can't manage that, the Iron Way will hear of it. And we have... ways... of settling disputes when communities can't manage themselves."

He let the vague threat linger. He had no idea what the Iron

Way's actual dispute resolution methods were, but he figured something involving stern men on loud motorcycles probably wasn't far off the mark.

The effect was remarkable. Faced with a clear directive from an authority figure they dared not openly defy, and perhaps shamed by the obviousness of the solution they had failed to implement themselves, the animosity between the two families seemed to momentarily recede, replaced by a grudging acceptance.

Greerson looked at Henderson. Henderson looked at his wife, who gave a stiff nod. "Alright, Rider," Greerson said, his voice subdued. "We'll... we'll see to it."

Tweese stayed for another hour, watching them under the hot sun as they fetched their tools and, with much initial awkwardness and muttered complaints, began the work. He didn't lift a finger to help, merely observed from the seat of his motorcycle, the quiet thrum of the engine a subtle reminder of his presence. He was the catalyst, the adjudicator, not the laborer. It was a new role for him, and he found it fit surprisingly well. The ease with which they'd accepted his authority, the way their long-standing feud seemed to crumble before a few firm words and the implied might of the Iron Way, was... illuminating.

As the first significant branches were hacked away from the fallen tree and a muddy trickle of water began to snake its way further down the choked ditch, Mrs. Henderson approached him, wiping sweat from her brow with a grimy forearm. "Rider," she said, her earlier sharpness softened by exertion and a hesitant gratitude. "We... we ain't got much. But we'd be honored if you'd share our midday meal. Some stew, fresh-baked bread, what little we have."

Tweese considered. He still had provisions from Walsenberg. But a hot meal was a hot meal. And accepting their hospitality would further cement his role, his influence. "I'll accept." he said with a nod.

The meal was meager, but offered with genuine thanks. As he ate, sitting on a rough-hewn bench outside the Henderson's dilapidated farmhouse, he watched the two families, still working with a certain degree of sullenness but working *together*, to clear the waterway. He saw the first real surge of water begin to flow down the ditch. He heard the surprised, joyful shout from one of the Greerson boys.

He left an hour later, after the main trunk of the tree had been shifted and water was gushing, muddy but plentiful, down the newly cleared channel. Both families, exhausted and mud-spattered but with a new, fragile truce between them, offered him their thanks again. Greerson even pressed a small, carefully wrapped packet of dried apples into his hand. "For the road, Rider. And... our apologies for the trouble."

As Tweese rode away, the image of the two families working together, the sound of the flowing water, stayed with him. He'd done very little, really. Pointed out the obvious. Issued a few commands. The real work had been done by them. Yet, they treated him as if he'd performed some minor miracle. He felt a familiar satisfaction, the smooth click of a successful operation. But beneath it, there was something else, something harder to define. A sense of... efficacy? He'd spoken, and the world had shifted, just a little. And it had been surprisingly easy. Too easy, perhaps. He was succeeding, not because of any intrinsic heroism or wisdom on his part, he knew that. He was succeeding because of the jacket, the bike, and the desperate hunger these people had for any semblance of order, any figure of authority in a world that had precious little of either. He was a symbol, nothing more. And symbols, he was beginning to realize, could be powerful things indeed, even if the man embodying the symbol was a complete fraud.

The taste of dried apples and the faint, lingering scent

of woodsmoke from the Henderson's cookfire were pleasant memories as Tweese pushed further north on the I-25. The encounter with the feuding farmers had been... instructive. It had cost him little more than a few hours of his time, some stern posturing, and the recitation of a few well-chosen, authoritative-sounding phrases. In return, he'd received food, genuine gratitude, and, more importantly, another successful test of the Iron Way persona. The jacket and the bike were proving to be remarkably effective keys, unlocking doors of deference and cooperation that would have remained firmly shut to Phillip Tweese, lone scavenger.

He rode for another day, the landscape growing, if possible, even more desolate. The ruins he passed seemed older, more thoroughly picked over, the skeletal remains of towns and truck stops offering little more than windbreaks and shadows. The religious signs persisted, their stark white messages – "FIND SALVATION IN HIS LIGHT," "THE WAGES OF SIN ARE ASHES" – standing out against the muted canvas of the plains. Tweese wondered about the people who painted them, what kind of fervor or desperation drove them to such public declarations in a world that seemed largely indifferent to any god, old or new.

Late in the afternoon of the second day after leaving the farmers, as he was scouting for a place to make a cold camp for the night, he spotted a faint plume of smoke on the horizon, a thin, wavering finger against the bruised purple of the approaching dusk. Smoke usually meant people, and people usually meant complications. But people also meant potential resources, and his supplies from Walsenberg and the farmers wouldn't last forever. His curiosity, and the growing confidence in his assumed identity, got the better of his ingrained caution.

He approached slowly, the motorcycle's engine a low thrum that wouldn't carry too far on the evening air. The smoke, he soon saw, was coming from a small cluster of buildings huddled in a shallow depression a few miles off the main highway, barely visible until he was almost upon them. It wasn't much of a settlement: three or four ramshackle structures made of scavenged timber and corrugated iron, surrounded by a haphazard, poorly maintained fence of sharpened poles and tangled wire. A few scrawny goats, their ribs showing, bleated mournfully from a small, muddy enclosure.

As he neared, a figure detached itself from the largest building – a man, lean and weathered, carrying an old, long-barreled hunting rifle. He watched Tweese's approach with the same wary suspicion he'd encountered in Walsenberg, but there was a deeper weariness in his eyes, a haunted look that spoke of recent loss.

Tweese brought the bike to a halt a respectful distance away, cutting the engine. He pushed up his goggles. "Evening," he called out, his voice calm. "Just a traveler, looking for a place to rest my head for the night, if you're amenable. Got my own provisions."

The man's gaze flickered over the motorcycle, lingered on the Iron Way jacket. The tension in his shoulders eased almost imperceptibly. "Iron Way?" he asked, his voice raspy.

Tweese gave a noncommittal grunt that he hoped sounded affirmative. It had worked before. "Ain't seen your colors this far out in a long spell," the man said. He lowered his rifle slightly. "Name's Silas. This here is... well, it ain't much, but we call it Shepherd's Rest." A bitter twist of his lips accompanied the name. "Not much resting going on lately, though. And not much shepherding, neither."

"Trouble?" Tweese asked, keeping his tone neutral. He was getting a feel for this. Project authority, ask a leading question, let them fill in the blanks.

Silas sighed, a sound like dry leaves skittering across stone. "Trouble enough. Wolves. Got into the pen again last night. Took another two goats. Best milker and a young kid." His voice was flat, devoid of emotion, but his knuckles were white where he gripped the rifle. "That's four this week. We ain't got many left to lose."

"Wolves, you say?" Tweese looked around at the flimsy enclosure, the dilapidated fence. It wouldn't keep out a determined stray dog, let alone a pack of actual wolves. "Big ones?"

"Big enough," Silas said grimly. "And cunning. They come in the night, quiet as shadows. We barely hear 'em 'til it's too late, and by then..." He gestured vaguely towards a spot beyond the fence where the earth was disturbed. Tweese didn't need to see the remains to understand.

A woman emerged from the doorway of the main building, her face etched with worry. She carried a small, sputtering oil lamp that cast flickering, unreliable light on her drawn features. Two small children clung to her skirts, their eyes wide and fearful as they stared at Tweese.

"Silas? Is everything alright?" she asked, her voice thin.

"It's... it's an Iron Way rider, Martha-Anne," Silas replied, a note of something that might have been hope, or perhaps just desperate appeal, in his voice. "Maybe... maybe he can help us."

Martha-Anne looked at Tweese, her gaze traveling from his dusty boots to the imposing jacket, then to the powerful motorcycle. "Help us?" she echoed, as if the concept was foreign. "With the wolves?"

Tweese felt the familiar weight of expectation settle upon him. Wolves. He knew a little about wolves, mostly from old stories. They were smart, dangerous pack hunters. If this settlement was truly being preyed upon by a wolf pack, it was a serious problem, likely beyond his capabilities to solve with a bit of noise and bluster. But his success at Walsenberg, and with the feuding farmers, had bred a certain careless confidence. He was an Iron

Way rider, wasn't he? And Iron Way riders solved problems.

"Might be I could take a look," he said, echoing the words he'd used before. "See what you're up against." He was already calculating. A few dead goats weren't his concern, but a grateful community, however small and impoverished, might offer something – a bit more fuel, a meal, information. And the chance to play the hero again, to feel that strange, discomfiting but undeniably potent surge of respect, was a lure in itself, though he'd never admit it, even to himself.

The next morning, under a sky the color of a fresh bruise, Tweese began his "investigation." Silas, looking even more haggard in the daylight, led him to the goat pen. The scene was grim. Blood stained the muddy earth, and the pathetic, torn remains of one of the goats lay near a breach in the flimsy fence – a section where the wire had been pulled down and a couple of the sharpened poles knocked askew.

"See?" Silas said, his voice tight. "They just… tore right through. Like it was nothing."

Tweese knelt, examining the tracks in the mud around the pen. They were plentiful, but… they weren't wolf tracks. He'd seen drawings of wolf tracks in an old-world book once, in a display in some crumbling museum he'd picked through years ago in Houston, far south of here.

They were large, powerful, the claws non-retractable, leaving distinct impressions. These tracks were smaller, the claw marks less pronounced, more splayed. These were dog tracks. Large dogs, to be sure, but dogs nonetheless. Feral dogs, most likely, a pack that had reverted to their wilder instincts, driven by hunger. Dangerous, yes, but not the same as a coordinated wolf pack.

He then examined the "breach" in the fence. The wire was old and rusted, easily broken. The poles were rotted at the base, offering little resistance. It looked less like a determined assault by powerful predators and more like an opportunistic entry by animals that had discovered a particularly easy source of food.

"You're sure these are wolves?" Tweese asked, keeping his expression carefully neutral.

Silas looked at him, a flicker of defensiveness in his eyes. "What else would they be? They're killing our stock, ain't they? Big, grey shapes, seen 'em at a distance in the dusk. Howl at night, sometimes. Sounds like wolves to me."

Feral dogs could be grey. Feral dogs could howl. And feral dogs, if hungry enough, would certainly kill livestock. Tweese had encountered packs of them before in ruined cities, wary, cunning creatures - a menace to a solitary scavenger.

He spent some time walking the perimeter of the settlement, Silas trailing anxiously behind him. He noted the general state of disrepair, the lack of any real defensive planning. Shepherd's Rest was an open invitation to any predator, four-legged or two. Their problem wasn't just "wolves"; it was a fundamental failure to secure their own livelihood. Complacency, again. Or perhaps just a weariness so profound it had sapped their will to take even basic precautions.

"The tracks tell a story," Tweese said finally, adopting his serious, analytical tone. He'd learned that people were more inclined to believe you if you sounded like you knew things they didn't. "These aren't just random attacks. There's a pattern. They're testing your defenses, finding the weakest points." He pointed towards a section of the fence that was particularly dilapidated. "They'll likely try here again, or somewhere similar."

"So, what do we do?" Silas asked, his voice desperate. "Can you... can you hunt them down for us, Rider? Track them to their den?" He clearly envisioned Tweese as some legendary wasteland tracker, a lone hero venturing out to slay the monsters.

Tweese had no intention of tracking a pack of large, hungry feral dogs into their own territory. That was a good way to become dog food. His solution, as in Walsenberg, needed to be more about stagecraft and less about actual confrontation.

"Hunting them is one option," Tweese said slowly, as if weighing complex strategies. "But a pack like this, if it's established, killing a few might just make the rest more cunning, or another pack might move in. The better solution is to make Shepherd's Rest too difficult, too dangerous a target. We need to fortify. We need to show them this is no longer an easy meal."

Over the next few hours, much like he had in Walsenberg, Tweese directed Silas and a couple of other men from the settlement – there were only five adults in total, he discovered, and the other two were old and frail – in making rudimentary repairs to the goat pen and the outer fence.

He had them reinforce the poles, string new lengths of scavenged wire, and pile thorny bushes around the base of the fence to act as a further deterrent. It was basic, common-sense stuff they should have done from the start.

As they worked, Silas talked, a stream of grievances and worries. He spoke of better times, just a few years back, when there were more families at Shepherd's Rest, when the rains were more reliable, and when predators, animal or human, seemed to keep their distance. "It's not like we *wanted* things to get this way, Rider," Silas said, his voice low and defensive as he wrestled with a stubborn fence post. "Used to be, this place was... easier. We had more hands. Old Man Gable, he was sharp as a tack then, kept the fences mended proper. And the weather... it wasn't so damn mean. We figured being this far off the main roads, folks would mostly leave us be. You get busy with the day-to-day, you know? Planting, tending what little grows. You tell yourself the watch can be a bit looser tonight, the fence can wait another week. Then the dry season hits hard, a sickness takes a few good folk, and suddenly... suddenly the wolves are at the goats, and you're wondering how it all slipped away so fast."

Tweese listened, offering little in response beyond occasional grunts or nods. It was the same story he'd heard, in one variation or another, in countless other failing settlements. A slow slide, a series of small neglects and rationalizations, a belief that just getting by was enough, until a crisis hit and they found themselves unprepared, their skills atrophied, their will eroded. They hadn't so much chosen complacency as drifted into it, one small, unaddressed problem at a time.

When the physical work was done, the goat pen looking marginally more secure, Tweese outlined the second part of his plan. "Tonight," he said, gathering Silas and the other able-bodied man, a younger fellow named Caleb, "we don't just wait. We make it known that this place is protected."

His plan was similar to the one he'd used at the granary: noise, and the illusion of a strong, alert defense. He had them gather metal pots, pans, anything that would make a loud clang. He also had them build up the fire in the center of the settlement, making it larger and brighter than usual. "When it's full dark," he instructed, "we take turns on watch. Not just sitting by the fire, but walking the perimeter. And if we see anything, or hear anything, we don't hesitate. We make noise. Shout. Bang these pots. Let them know we're here, we're awake, and we're ready."

He also suggested they bring the remaining goats into the largest, most secure building for the night, an idea that seemed revolutionary to Silas. "Inside?" Silas had asked, blinking. "With us?" "Better than leaving them out as bait," Tweese had replied dryly.

That night, Tweese took the first watch. He walked the perimeter of Shepherd's Rest, the motorcycle parked near the central fire, a silent but potent symbol of his supposed authority. He carried his .45 openly, though he still had no intention of using it unless absolutely necessary. The night was cold and quiet, the only sounds the bleating of the goats now safely (and rather smellily) ensconced in the main building, and the crackle of the fire.

Around midnight, he saw them – a pair of shadowy figures, low to the ground, moving with a furtive grace at the edge of the firelight, their eyes glinting like hot coals. Feral dogs, just as he'd suspected. Large, gaunt, their ribs visible even in the dim light. They were testing the air, sniffing towards the now-empty goat pen.

Tweese didn't hesitate. He let out a sharp, barking shout and banged the metal cup he was carrying against a fence post with a loud clang. Silas and Caleb, startled awake by the sudden noise, quickly joined in, shouting and banging their own improvised noisemakers. The dogs, surprised by the sudden, aggressive display from a place they'd likely come to regard as an easy buffet, froze for a moment, then turned and melted back into the darkness.

They repeated the performance twice more before dawn, as other shadowy figures tested the settlement's new alertness. Each time, the immediate, noisy response sent the dogs fleeing. No shots were fired, no actual confrontation occurred. It was all bluff and bluster.

By morning, the settlers of Shepherd's Rest were exhausted but elated. No goats had been taken. The "wolves" had been repelled. Their savior, the Iron Way rider, had once again proven his worth. Silas pressed a small, greasy jar of what he claimed was good-quality fat-fuel into Tweese's hand – less than he'd hoped for, but Silas swore it was all they could spare. Martha-Anne gave him a hunk of dry, hard bread and a waterskin filled with clean, if slightly metallic-tasting, water.

As Tweese prepared to leave, the familiar scene of gratitude played out. Silas wrung his hand, Caleb nodded with shy respect, and the children stared with wide, wondering eyes. "Well, Rider," Silas said, his voice thick with emotion, though a hint of his earlier weariness still clung to him. "You certainly stirred things up. Haven't had a night like that in... ever, I reckon. Those... things... they won't be bothering us again soon, not after that racket." He managed a thin smile. "Good to know there's still folks like the Iron Way out there, looking out."

Tweese nodded, accepting their thanks with a practiced air of stoic competence. He was getting very good at playing this part. And as he rode away from Shepherd's Rest, the small, struggling settlement already shrinking in his mirrors, he felt that now-familiar sense of satisfaction. Another problem "solved." Another community "saved." His reputation, or rather, the reputation of the man they thought him to be, was growing with each encounter.

Usually, when he left a place, he was looking over his shoulder, half-expecting shouts of anger or the thud of a well-aimed rock once his deceptions unraveled or his pilfered goods were missed. This was different. There was no landmine left behind here, no ticking clock until discovery. These people would remember the "Iron Way rider" with gratitude, not curses. It was a novel sensation, leaving a place better than he'd found it, even if the method was pure theater. He wouldn't have admitted it to anyone, least of all himself, but there was a certain pragmatic appeal to it. A string of welcoming settlements to his south, places he could theoretically return to if things went sour further north... it wasn't a bad thing to have in your back pocket. A con man always appreciated a good bolt-hole, even if he never intended to use it.

He was still a fraud, of course. A scavenger in a stolen jacket, playing a role for fuel and food. But the ease with which these communities accepted his authority, the almost desperate way they clung to the illusion of strength he projected, was making him think. He was learning that the appearance of power, in a world starved of it, could be almost as effective as the real thing. And he was learning that even the simplest, most obvious solutions seemed like miracles to people who had forgotten how to solve their own problems. It was a dangerous lesson, one that was slowly, almost imperceptibly, beginning to change the way Phillip Tweese saw himself, and the broken world around him.

The jar of fat-fuel from Silas, though meager, was enough to get Tweese another fifty or sixty miles north along the decaying scar of the I-25. Shepherd's Rest, with its grateful, frightened inhabitants and their easily cowed feral dogs, was already a fading memory, another notch on the handle of his increasingly effective Iron Way persona. Each successful intervention, each community left slightly better off (or at least, less immediately threatened) than he'd found them, added a subtle layer to his confidence. He was still Phillip Tweese, scavenger and opportunist, underneath the heavy leather jacket, but the role of the competent, authoritative Rider was beginning to feel less like a costume and more like a second skin – a very useful, resource-generating second skin.

He rode through a landscape that seemed to grow more barren with each passing mile. The skeletal ruins of overpasses loomed like forgotten monuments to a grander, busier age. The plains stretched out, vast and indifferent, under a sky that was often a pale, washed-out blue, or a threatening, bruised grey. The religious signs continued their silent, persistent commentary by the roadside: "THE PATH TO DAMNATION IS WIDE," one proclaimed in stark white letters on a sheet of rusted metal; "ONLY THE RIGHTEOUS SHALL ENDURE," screamed another from the side of a collapsed grain silo. Tweese found himself looking for them now, almost expecting them around each bend. *Where in the blazes are they even getting all that white paint?* he wondered. *And who's got the time and organization to keep slapping these things up across this much empty country?* It wasn't just a couple of isolated messages anymore; it felt like a deliberate, widespread campaign. It was a con of a different sort, he mused, though what they were selling, and to whom, wasn't immediately clear. Faith was a powerful motivator, he knew that much. It could also be a powerful tool for control. He filed the thought away, another piece of the strange puzzle of this new territory.

It was late afternoon, the sun beginning its slow descent and painting the western sky in fiery hues, when he spotted a flicker of movement ahead, just off the main highway. It wasn't much, just a couple of dilapidated structures clustered around what looked like a hand-dug well and a few struggling, dust-choked trees – an oasis of sorts, if your standards for an oasis were pitifully low.

A thin, hopeful tendril of smoke curled upwards from a rusty stovepipe chimney. This was Bitter Springs, according to a crudely painted sign half-buried in the dirt. Tweese saw plenty that looked bitter, but nothing that resembled a spring. More like Bitter Puddle, he thought. The air here felt drier, the silence deeper, a profound quietude underscored by the drone of insects and the distant caw of a crow. He could smell dust, a hint of woodsmoke, and the faint, skunky tang of stagnant water.

As he approached, the details sharpened. The shacks were cobbled together from mismatched planks, sheets of rusted tin, and what looked like old vehicle panels, all leaning at precarious angles. The "well" was a muddy hole with a rickety windlass. The trees were stunted, their leaves coated in a fine layer of ochre dust. He saw it was a tiny, almost comically vulnerable attempt at a roadside stop. A single, rickety table displayed a few pathetic offerings: a couple of dusty, shriveled-looking gourds that might have been squash once, a small pile of what might have been dried herbs tied with string, and three chipped ceramic mugs.

An older woman, her face a roadmap of wrinkles and worry, her knuckles swollen, sat on a crate behind the table, her hands clasped tightly in her lap. She watched his approach with wide, apprehensive eyes, the kind that had seen too much trouble and expected more. A younger man, probably her son, rail-thin and with a nervous, hunted look about him, was attempting to draw water from the well, his movements jerky and inefficient, the frayed rope slipping in his grasp. He kept glancing over his shoulder, not at Tweese, but at the larger of the two shacks.

Tweese slowed the motorcycle, his senses on alert. Small, isolated outposts like this were often targets, their very vulnerability an invitation. He saw the woman's head snap up fully as he got closer, her eyes widening with alarm. The young man at the well finally noticed him, dropped the bucket with a clatter into the muddy water, and reached for a rusty tire iron that lay nearby, brandishing it with more fear than conviction.

Before Tweese could even offer a greeting, his usual opening line about being a weary traveler already forming on his lips, another figure emerged from the larger of the two shacks – a burly, unkempt man with a greasy beard that looked like it housed its own ecosystem, and a swagger that suggested he owned the place, or at least thought he did. He wore a collection of mismatched scavenged clothing – a faded military-style jacket over a stained undershirt, patched trousers of differing materials – and a heavy, crudely made club, its head wrapped in barbed wire, was thrust through a loop in his belt. He was followed by a second, slightly smaller but equally thuggish-looking individual, this one with a nervous tic that made his left eye twitch.

The burly man swaggered towards the table, ignoring Tweese for the moment, his heavy boots kicking up dust. He picked up one of the shriveled gourds, sniffed it disdainfully, then tossed it back onto the table where it landed with a dull thud. "Slim pickings today, Agnes," he said, his voice a gravelly sneer that seemed to vibrate with menace. "The Bitter Springs toll ain't gonna pay itself with this rabbit food. Barely enough here to feed a sick rat."

The old woman, Agnes, flinched but held her ground, though

her clasped hands tightened until her knuckles were white. "We ain't had many travelers, Corbin," she said, her voice thin but defiant, like a dry reed in the wind. "And the well's been slow. Not much to offer. You know how it is."

"Not much to offer?" Corbin laughed, a harsh, unpleasant sound that made the crows in the dusty trees take flight. "You always got something to offer, Agnes. Always. Maybe young Davey here can offer up some of that water he's so slow at drawing. Looks like he's about to spill half of it anyway." He gestured with his chin towards the well. "Or perhaps a bit of... company... from the back room, eh, for a thirsty man?" He leered at Agnes, a grotesque twisting of his features, and his companion snickered, a wet, gurgling sound.

Davey, the young man, took a shaky step forward, the tire iron held awkwardly in his hand, a symbol of defiance more than a credible threat. "Leave her alone, Corbin! We paid our due last week! You took the last of the jerky!"

Corbin turned on him, his smile vanishing, replaced by a look of pure malice. "Paid your due? You call that handful of dried weeds and a few strips of mystery-meat paying your due? This is *my* spring, Davey-boy. My road. This waterhole, these shacks, they exist because *I* allow it. Anyone wants to use it, anyone wants to sell their pathetic wares beside it, they pay Corbin. That's the law around here. My law." He took a menacing step towards Davey, who flinched but didn't back down, though his grip on the tire iron tightened. Corbin's companion shifted, his hand going to a long knife tucked into his belt.

Tweese had seen enough. This wasn't a raid by desperate scavs; this was simple, thuggish extortion by a couple of local bullies who had clearly terrorized these poor folk into submission. It was a petty tyranny, a microcosm of the larger brutalities of the wasteland, but for Agnes and Davey, it was likely a constant source of fear and misery. And it was, he realized with a familiar stirring of opportunistic calculation, another perfect stage for the Iron Way rider. This was almost too easy.

He let the motorcycle's engine idle for another moment, its quiet thrum a subtle announcement of his presence, a sound that was beginning to cut through the tension. Then, he deliberately goosed the throttle. The sudden, sharp bark of the diesel engine made all four of them jump and turn towards him, their petty drama momentarily forgotten. He rode the bike slowly forward, the tires crunching on the dry, gravelly earth, stopping a few feet from Corbin, who now looked less like a swaggering bully and more like a startled badger caught out in the open.

Tweese scrubbed a hand over his dusty face, pushing back a stray lock of hair, his expression set in what he hoped was an expression of cold, implacable authority. He let his gaze sweep over Corbin and his twitchy crony, then to Agnes and Davey, who were staring at him with a mixture of fear and dawning, fragile hope, then back to Corbin. He didn't say a word, letting the silence and the presence of the bike do the talking for him.

The silence stretched, thick and heavy. Corbin, clearly unnerved by the sudden appearance of a heavily armored man on a powerful, well-maintained motorcycle, shifted his weight uneasily from one foot to the other. His bravado seemed to be rapidly evaporating, like water on hot stone. His companion looked like he was about to wet himself. "Who... who the hell are you?" Corbin finally managed, his voice a good deal less confident than it had been moments before, the sneer replaced by a quaver of uncertainty.

"Here for the toll," Tweese said, his voice flat and hard, each word dropping like a stone. Corbin blinked, his greasy forehead wrinkling in confusion. "The toll? *I* collect the toll around here. This is my..." "Not anymore," Tweese cut him off, his voice like a whip crack. "The Iron Way has an interest in this road. And we don't appreciate... unregulated commerce. Or bullies preying on settlers." He let his hand drift towards the butt of the .45 beneath his jacket. He didn't draw it, didn't even touch it, but the gesture, slow and deliberate, was unmistakable.

Corbin's eyes widened. He'd clearly heard of the Iron Way. Few people along this stretch of the I-25 corridor hadn't. Their reputation for ruthless efficiency in dealing with those who disrupted their operations, or those who claimed territory the Way considered its own, was legendary, often embellished in the telling but rooted in a very real capacity for violence. "Iron... Iron Way?" Corbin stammered, his face paling to a sickly grey beneath the grime. His companion took an involuntary step back, looking ready to bolt. "Look, friend, Rider... there's no need for trouble. We were just... just having a bit of a chat with old Agnes here. A misunderstanding. No harm done."

"Looked like more than a chat to me," Tweese said, his gaze unwavering, pinning Corbin like an insect. "Looked like extortion. And the Iron Way doesn't tolerate extortion on roads under its protection." He was making this up as he went along, tailoring the Iron Way's supposed policies to the situation at hand, but it sounded convincing, even to his own ears. The settlers at Walsenberg and Shepherd's Rest had been so quick to believe; these two thugs looked even more susceptible to the power of reputation.

"No, no, you got it all wrong, Rider," Corbin said quickly, holding up his hands in a placating gesture, palms out. "We're... we're just local boys. Just looking out for our own. Agnes, Davey, they're... they're friends. Good neighbors. Ain't that right, Agnes?" He shot a desperate, pleading look at the old woman, his eyes begging her to play along.

Agnes, who had been watching the exchange with a mixture of terror and dawning, almost disbelieving hope, found her voice. It was thin, like old parchment, but it carried a surprising strength. "They... they ain't no friends of ours, Rider," she said, her voice trembling but clear, her gaze fixed on Tweese. "They take what little we have. Threaten us. Make our lives a misery."

Tweese looked back at Corbin, his expression like stone. "Seems Agnes has a different understanding of your 'friendship'." Corbin's bluster completely collapsed. He looked from Tweese's unyielding face to the powerful motorcycle, its polished chrome glinting in the fading sun, to the ominous bulk of the armored jacket. He was clearly outmatched and outmaneuvered, and he knew it. The calculation was plain on his face: fight and likely die, or run and live to bully someone else, somewhere else. "Look, Rider, maybe... maybe we made a mistake," Corbin mumbled, his eyes darting around for an escape route, no longer meeting Tweese's. "A misunderstanding. No harm, no foul, right? We'll just... we'll just be on our way. Leave these good folks in peace. No more trouble from us, swear on... on whatever you like."

"You'll do more than that," Tweese said, his voice cold. He pointed with a gloved finger to the meager offerings on Agnes's table, then to the greasy pouch on Corbin's belt. "You'll compensate them for the 'tolls' you've already collected. All of it. And then you'll get out of Bitter Springs. And if I, or any other Iron Way rider, hear that you're troubling these people, or anyone else along this stretch, again..." He let the threat hang, unfinished but potent, letting Corbin's own fearful imagination fill in the grisly details.

Corbin and his crony didn't need further encouragement. With fumbling haste, his hands shaking, Corbin unhooked the greasy pouch from his belt and tossed it onto the table. It landed with a dull thud, heavier than Tweese had expected. He then grabbed his companion by the arm, and the two of them practically stumbled over each other in their eagerness to retreat, disappearing back into the shack they'd emerged from. Moments later, they burst out the back and scurried away into the scrubland like startled rats, not even daring to look back.

Silence descended again, punctuated only by the quiet idling of Tweese's motorcycle and Davey's ragged breathing. Agnes and Davey stared at him, their faces a study in disbelief and overwhelming relief. "They... they're gone?" Davey whispered, as if he couldn't quite believe it, his grip on the tire iron finally loosening. "For now," Tweese said. "And they'll stay gone, if they've got any sense."

Agnes approached him then, her wrinkled hands clasped before her, her movements slow but determined. "Rider... I... we don't know how to thank you. Corbin... he's been a plague on us for months. We... we had no way to stop him." Tears welled in her eyes, tracing clean paths through the dust on her cheeks. "You... you're a true Knight of the Road."

Tweese felt that familiar, discomfiting warmth spread through him, a sensation he was beginning to recognize, though not yet understand. A Knight of the Road. It was a far cry from the truth. He was just a scavenger, a drifter, who'd stumbled into a good jacket and an even better story. But that was the power of a good story, wasn't it? It could make people believe, make them hope, even change the way they saw the world, if only for a little while. It could certainly make bullies turn tail.

"Just keeping the roads clear," he said, his voice gruffer than he intended, trying to deflect the intensity of her gaze. "The Iron Way expects peace." Davey, his earlier fear replaced by a hesitant admiration, shyly offered him water from the well – cool and surprisingly sweet, a welcome relief from the dust of the road. Agnes pressed one of the shriveled gourds into his hand. "It ain't much, Rider, but it's all we have to offer. Please, take it. For your kindness."

He accepted their meager gifts. He knew they had little, and he had his own supplies. But refusing would have been... ungracious. And the role he was playing, the role of the benevolent, if stern, protector, seemed to demand a certain noblesse oblige, didn't it? He didn't stay long at Bitter Springs. There was no fuel to be had beyond what Corbin had unwittingly "donated" (which Agnes insisted he take, along with the contents of the pouch, a collection of small, worn pre-collapse coins and a few shiny buttons – more than he'd expected), and he had miles to cover before nightfall. But as he rode away, leaving the two grateful settlers waving shyly after him, the setting sun casting their small figures in long, lonely shadows, he reflected on the encounter. It had been almost laughably easy. Two local bullies, puffed up with their own petty power, had crumbled at the mere sight of him, at the mere mention of the Iron Way.

His confidence, already bolstered by his successes in Walsenberg and with the feuding farmers, swelled a little further. This Iron Way gig, it was working out even better than he'd hoped. People were so easily intimidated, so eager to believe in a strong hand, a protector. He was providing a service, of a sort. He was solving their little problems, making their lives a bit easier. And in return, he was getting what he needed to survive, and more. He was getting respect. He was building a network of... well, not exactly friends, but grateful acquaintances. Places he could, in theory, fall back to if his push north didn't pan out. It was a strange new way of operating, leaving behind a wake of goodwill instead of suspicion and hastily covered tracks. He wasn't sure he liked the feeling, not entirely. It felt... complicated. But he couldn't deny its effectiveness.

The wasteland was a harsh place, but maybe, just maybe, he'd found a new way to navigate its dangers, a way that involved more than just looking out for himself. Or maybe, he was just getting better at a more sophisticated kind of con. He wasn't sure which it was. But as long as it kept his fuel tank full and his belly from aching, he figured he'd keep playing the part.

CHAPTER 4: THE SANCTUARY OF THE DIVINE SPARK

The small comforts and easy victories of Shepherd's Rest and Bitter Springs were now several days behind him. Phillip Tweese pushed the motorcycle north, the landscape becoming increasingly scarred and desolate as he drew nearer to the rumored desolation of what had once been Denver. The I-25 was a treacherous beast here, great chunks of asphalt missing like rotten teeth, often forcing him to slow to a crawl or navigate long, bumpy detours through the parched scrubland that pressed in on either side. The fat-fuel he'd acquired, while keeping the engine running, was clearly taking its toll. The bike had begun to sputter intermittently, coughing black, greasy smoke, and the usually smooth thrum of its diesel heart now carried an occasional, worrying hiccup. He knew enough about engines – a skill picked up from countless hours tinkering with scavenged junk – to recognize the signs of a clogged fuel line or a fouled filter. The impure, poorly rendered fats were leaving their mark.

He needed cleaner fuel, and soon. And a new filter, if he could find one. The thought of Denver loomed large and unpleasant in his mind. He'd heard the stories: a sprawling ruin ruled by the iron fist of the Buffalo Boys, a place where life was cheap and outsiders, especially anyone even vaguely resembling a rival faction, were met with swift and brutal violence. The Iron Way jacket, which had been his golden ticket through the smaller settlements, would be a death sentence there.

The religious signs became more frequent, more elaborate. No longer just simple, stark messages on rusted metal, some were now larger, painted on relatively intact sections of old billboards or the sides of crumbling overpasses. "THE DIVINE SPARK RESIDES IN THE RIGHTEOUS HEART!" one declared in surprisingly neat lettering. Another, near a particularly grim-looking ruin that might have been a pre-collapse truck stop, offered: "LOST? AFRAID? LET THE SPARK GUIDE YOU TO SANCTUARY!" They were too well-maintained, too consistent in their style, to be the work of isolated madmen. This was an organized effort. *Someone's putting a lot of resources into this,* Tweese thought, his cynicism piqued. *Paint, brushes, manpower to get to these high places… what's the payoff? What are they selling? Hope's a cheap commodity to manufacture, but it usually comes with a high price for the buyer.*

His bike coughed again, a violent, shuddering spasm that almost stalled the engine. He cursed under his breath, easing off the throttle. He was losing power, and the next settlement marked on his tattered, scavenged map – a place called "Harmony Glade" according to the faded ink – was still a good day's ride, assuming the map was even accurate. Denver was closer, but infinitely more dangerous. He scanned the horizon, looking for any sign of shelter or opportunity.

As he crested a low rise, his survey of the empty horizon was broken by an unexpected sight. It wasn't Harmony Glade, but something far more imposing, something that wasn't on his map at all. In the distance, perhaps five or six miles off the main highway, nestled in a shallow valley and catching the harsh afternoon sun, was a massive, sprawling complex of buildings.

Even from this far, he could see high walls, watchtowers, and a central structure that rose above the others, its architecture strangely familiar from pictures he'd seen in scavenged pre-collapse books – a megachurch. But unlike the ruins he was accustomed to, this place looked... intact. Maintained. There was even a faint haze above it that might be smoke from numerous chimneys, or perhaps even the output of some kind of small-scale industry. And leading towards it, branching off the I-25, was a secondary road, dusty but clearly used. One of the prominent religious signs, larger than any he'd seen before, stood at the turnoff: "THE SANCTUARY OF THE DIVINE SPARK WELCOMES ALL WHO SEEK THE LIGHT. TURN HERE FOR REFUGE AND RENEWAL."

Refuge and Renewal, Tweese thought. *Or a really well-organized con.* His bike sputtered again, more weakly this time. He was running out of options. Denver was a death trap. Pushing on towards Harmony Glade on a failing machine was a fool's errand. This "Sanctuary," whatever it was, looked like it had resources. And where there were resources, there was usually a way for a man like Phillip Tweese to acquire some of them. He just had to figure out the angle.

He turned the motorcycle onto the secondary road, the engine complaining with every revolution. The road was better maintained than the interstate, the worst of the potholes filled with packed earth. As he drew closer, the sheer scale of the Sanctuary became apparent. The outer walls were high and sturdy, built of stone and reinforced timber, topped with sharpened stakes and what looked like makeshift guard posts manned by watchful figures. Inside, he could see rows of cultivated land – actual green, growing things, a rare and startling sight in this blighted landscape. Neatly laid out buildings, their roofs intact and showing signs of recent repair, were arranged around the massive central church structure, which gleamed with what might have been a fresh coat of whitewash. There was an air of order, of industry, of...

prosperity, almost. It was deeply unsettling. Places this well-organized, this self-sufficient, usually had very strict rules, and very little tolerance for outsiders who didn't fit in.

Two men, dressed in simple, clean, homespun tunics and trousers of a uniform pale grey, stood guard at a heavy wooden gate set into the main wall. They carried sturdy-looking staves, but their expressions were calm, almost serene, as Tweese approached. This was different from the wary, armed-to-the-teeth settlers he'd encountered so far. There was no visible fear in their eyes, only a quiet watchfulness.

He brought the bike to a halt, the engine dying with a final, pathetic cough. He was definitely not riding this thing any further without some serious attention. "Greetings, traveler," one of the guards said, his voice surprisingly gentle, yet firm. "You seek the light of the Spark?" Tweese ran a hand over his dusty face, his mind racing. The Iron Way persona might not play well here. These didn't look like people who would be easily intimidated. He decided on a modified approach: still the weary traveler, but perhaps less the enforcer. He certainly wouldn't be flashing the jacket or mentioning the Iron Way unless absolutely necessary. "Name's Phil," he said. "Bike's given up on me. Looking for a place to make repairs, maybe trade for some cleaner fuel, if you've got any to spare."

The guards exchanged a look, a silent communication that spoke of practiced routine. "All are welcome at the Sanctuary if they come in peace and with an open heart," the first guard said. "But we are a community of faith, traveler. Our resources are dedicated to the work of the Spark, and to those who embrace its teachings." *Here it comes,* Tweese thought. *The price of admission. Nothing's ever free.* "We have mechanics, of a sort," the second guard added, his gaze calm and steady. "Brother Zachary is skilled with engines when the Spark guides his hands. And our larders are, through the grace of the Spark, usually full. Pastor Eli is a generous man to those who are sincere in their hearts and willing to contribute to the community's harmony."

"Pastor Eli?" Tweese asked, feigning polite curiosity. "Our shepherd," the first guard said, a note of genuine reverence in his voice. "He guides us in the light. He brought the truth of the Spark to us when all was darkness. Perhaps you would speak with him? He often has wisdom to share with travelers who find their way to our gates, especially those whose journey has been hard."

Tweese considered. A direct confrontation or demand for resources was clearly out. These people were too organized, too self-assured. But if he played along, feigned an interest in their "Spark," he might gain access, assess their setup, find an opportunity. "I'd be willing to listen to any man who offers wisdom," he said, trying to sound humble and open-minded, a difficult stretch for him. He needed that fuel filter, and their "mechanics" were his best shot.

The guards seemed pleased by his amenable tone. They opened the gate, revealing a surprisingly clean and well-ordered courtyard. People moved about with a quiet sense of purpose – tending small, meticulously kept garden plots, repairing tools at a communal workshop, carrying water from a large cistern. There was none of the desperate, hand-to-mouth tension he'd seen in other settlements. Children, also dressed in simple grey, played a quiet game in a designated area, their laughter muted. It was... peaceful. Disturbingly so. The sheer level of organization was unlike anything he'd encountered outside of whispered tales of the Iron Way's strongholds.

He was led to a modest but well-constructed building near the central church, its door painted with a stylized, radiating sun symbol – the Spark, presumably. Pastor Eli, when he emerged, was not what Tweese had expected. He wasn't a wild-eyed fanatic or a bejeweled charlatan draped in scavenged finery. He was a man in late middle age, with kind, intelligent eyes that seemed to see right through a man, a neatly trimmed grey beard, and a calm, reassuring demeanor. He wore the same simple, homespun clothing as the others, though his was perhaps a little cleaner, a little less patched. He radiated an aura of quiet authority and genuine warmth that was, to Tweese, far more disarming than any overt display of power. *This one's good,* Tweese thought, his internal grifter-alarm bells ringing faintly but persistently. *Very good. The best ones always look harmless.*

"Welcome, brother," Pastor Eli said, his voice a rich, soothing baritone that seemed to vibrate with sincerity. He extended a hand, his grip firm and dry. "It is a hard road that brings travelers to our door. What troubles you, and how can the Sanctuary of the Divine Spark offer you solace and aid?"

Tweese explained his situation – the failing bike, the sputtering engine, his desperate need for a fuel filter and some cleaner burning fuel. He kept his tone respectful, that of a man seeking aid, not demanding it. He emphasized his willingness to trade or work for any assistance. He didn't mention the Iron Way, didn't flash the jacket. He was just Phil, a traveler in need, hoping their charity extended to mechanical failures. Pastor Eli listened patiently, his head tilted slightly, his gaze never leaving Tweese's face. He nodded occasionally, as if understanding not just the words but the unspoken weariness behind them. "The world outside our walls is indeed harsh, filled with broken things and broken spirits," he said when Tweese had finished. "Many lose their way, their inner Spark dimmed by hardship and despair. Here, we strive to rekindle that Spark, through honest labor, communal support, and a turning towards the light that resides within us all."

He paused, his gaze searching Tweese's face, and for a moment, Tweese felt like the Pastor could see every con he'd ever pulled, every lie he'd ever told. "We can offer you food and shelter for a time, brother Phil. Our Brother Zachary, who tends our generator and the old water pump, will look at your machine. He has a gift for such things. We ask only that you share in our work while you are with us – there is always much to be done – and open your heart to the possibility that the Spark may have guided you here for a reason greater than a broken fuel line."

It was a soft sell, but a sell nonetheless. Work for his keep, and listen to their sermons. Fair enough, on the surface. But Tweese knew there was always a catch, always a ledger being kept. He looked around at the orderly community, the productive gardens, the well-maintained buildings. This didn't happen by accident. It required resources, dedication, and a compliant workforce. He wondered how much of the "Spark" was genuine faith, and how much was a carefully crafted system for ensuring that compliance.

"I'm grateful for your offer, Pastor," Tweese said, managing a sincere-sounding tone. "I'm willing to earn my keep. And I'm always willing to learn." *Especially about how a setup this smooth operates, and where the real currency flows,* he added silently.

Pastor Eli smiled, a warm, benevolent expression that didn't quite reach his eyes, or so Tweese imagined. There was a shrewdness there, a keen intelligence that missed little. "Excellent, brother Phil. Excellent. Brother Thomas here," he gestured to one of the guards who had remained nearby, "will show you to a cot in the travelers' dormitory. We share what we have. And then, perhaps, you will join us for evening Repentance and Renewal. It is a balm for the weary soul, and a chance for the community to share its burdens and its joys."

The "travelers' dormitory" was a long, low building, cleaner than any place Tweese had slept in years. It held a dozen simple rope cots, each with a neatly folded grey blanket. Only a few were occupied by other quiet, weary-looking travelers. He was assigned a cot and left to himself for a few hours. He used the time to observe. From the small window of the dormitory, he could see the ceaseless, quiet industry of the Sanctuary. People moved with a purpose that was almost unnerving. There was no shouting, no arguments, just a steady rhythm of work – tending fields that stretched within the walls, repairing structures, carting supplies. Children attended an open-air lesson, their voices reciting something in unison. It was a picture of communal harmony, yet Tweese couldn't shake the feeling that he was looking at a well-managed ant colony.

The evening service of "Repentance and Renewal" was held in the main church, a cavernous space that, despite its size, felt intimate in the flickering light of hundreds of tallow candles. The air was thick with the smell of pine-incense and unwashed bodies, but also with an almost palpable fervor. Members of the community, "Brothers" and "Sisters" as they called each other, stood to give testimonials. They spoke of lives lost to scavenging, violence, and despair before finding the Sanctuary and Pastor Eli. They spoke of the "Divine Spark" awakening within them, bringing peace, purpose, and a sense of belonging. Their stories were emotional, often tearful, and the congregation responded with murmurs of "Praise the Spark" and "Amen, brother/sister."

Tweese listened, his cynicism warring with a reluctant fascination. Were these people genuinely transformed? Or were they expertly coached, their testimonies part of the indoctrination? Pastor Eli presided, his voice a soothing balm, interjecting with words of encouragement, parables about the Spark, and gentle exhortations to embrace communal love and reject the "selfish darkness of the Wasted World." He never raised his voice, yet his presence dominated the hall. He spoke of the Sanctuary as a beacon, a last hope in a fallen age, built on shared labor and shared faith. He also spoke, subtly but unmistakably, of the need for vigilance against "those who would dim the Spark," and the importance of contributing one's all to the community's strength.

After the service, a surprisingly substantial meal was served in a communal dining hall. Instead of the thin, watery broths and dried, stringy meat that had been his usual fare, the long tables were laden with platters of roasted root vegetables glistening with some kind of fat, thick slices of a dark, heavy bread that actually tasted of grain, and even bowls of what appeared to be a savory pottage with chunks of actual, identifiable cooked rabbit.

For the first time in what felt like an eternity, Tweese saw a communal meal that spoke of genuine surplus, not just shared scarcity. People spoke in low, earnest tones around him, the clatter of wooden bowls and spoons a comforting sound. There was a sense of order, of shared purpose, that was both impressive and, to him, deeply alien. He tried to engage a few of them in casual conversation, asking about their lives, about the Sanctuary. Their answers were invariably polite, but always circled back to Pastor Eli and the transformative power of the Spark. It was like they were all reading from the same script.

The next day, he was assigned to work alongside "Brother Zachary" in the workshop where they maintained the community's generator – an old, chugging diesel beast – and various other pieces of scavenged machinery. This Zachary was a quiet, capable man with grease-stained hands and an air of focused competence. He seemed less overtly devout than some of the others, more interested in the practical mechanics of keeping things running. "Your machine," Brother Zachary said, wiping his hands on a rag as he looked over Tweese's motorcycle, which had been wheeled into the workshop. "The fuel you've been using... it's like trying to run a fine watch on mud. Clogged the lines, fouled the filter something fierce."

"Can you fix it?" Tweese asked, trying to keep the desperation out of his voice.

Brother Zachary nodded slowly. "The Spark guides our hands to mend what is broken, be it a soul or an engine," he recited, the words sounding a bit practiced. He then added, more practically, "And call me Zach. Only the Pastor is so formal. We can flush the lines. We might have a filter that fits, or one we can adapt. We even refine some of our own fuel here, cleaner than what you'll find on the road. But these things take time, and resources,

Brother Phil." The implication was clear.

Tweese spent the day "assisting" Zach, which mostly involved handing him tools and trying to look useful. He also spent it asking careful, indirect questions about the Sanctuary. How did they get so much done? Where did their supplies come from? Who decided how things were run? Zach was guarded, but a few details emerged. The community tithed a significant portion of everything they produced – food, crafted goods, scavenged materials – to the "Storehouse of the Spark," which was managed directly by Pastor Eli and his closest "Elders." Labor was communal and assigned daily. Decisions, Zach said, were made by Pastor Eli, "guided by the wisdom of the Spark."

Tweese saw it clearly now. It *was* a racket, albeit a highly effective one. Pastor Eli was at the top of a pyramid, controlling the resources and the labor of a dedicated, faithful, and largely unquestioning workforce. But then, as he watched Zach expertly coax a sputtering water pump back to life, or saw the genuine relief on a woman's face when she received a share of the day's harvest, he had to admit, it *worked*. These people were fed, they were sheltered, they had a purpose. Their lives, however controlled, were demonstrably better than the desperate, hand-to-mouth existence of most folks he'd encountered in the Wasted World.

Was it exploitation if the exploited seemed content, even grateful? Was it a con if it provided genuine security and a measure of peace in a world that offered precious little of either? The questions gnawed at him. His own methods of survival suddenly felt crude, almost amateurish, compared to the sophisticated, large-scale operation Pastor Eli was running.

By the end of the second day, Zach declared the motorcycle's fuel line flushed and a scavenged, cleaned filter fitted. "She'll run better now, Brother Phil," he said. "And Pastor Eli has approved a small measure of our refined fuel for your journey, as a blessing of the Spark for your contribution to our labors." The "contribution" had been minimal, mostly hauling and fetching. The "blessing" was likely just enough fuel to get him well away from their gates. Tweese understood the unspoken message. He was an outsider, a potential disruption to their carefully balanced system. They had helped him, as their faith dictated, but they were not inviting him to stay.

As he prepared to leave the next morning, Pastor Eli met him at the gate, that same benevolent, unreadable smile on his face. "May the Spark light your path, Brother Phil," the Pastor said. "And may you find the peace and purpose that awaits all who truly seek it." "Thanks for the help, Pastor," Tweese said, keeping his tone neutral. He had his fuel, his filter. He'd learned a few things. It was time to go. "Remember, brother," Pastor Eli added, his eyes holding Tweese's for a moment. "The Sanctuary's gates are always open to those who wish to lay down their burdens and embrace the communal light."

Tweese nodded, catching the unspoken meaning clear as day. The gates were always open, sure, but the price of entry was to "embrace the communal light"—to bend the knee, to become another cog in Eli's well-oiled machine. It wasn't an invitation; it was a statement of terms. *Get out,* the Pastor's kind eyes seemed to say, *and don't come back unless you're ready to be broken and remade in our image.* He swung his leg over the bike and started the engine. It caught immediately, purring with a smooth, healthy rhythm that was a vast improvement. He gave a curt nod to Pastor Eli and the guards, then rode out of the Sanctuary of the Divine Spark, leaving its unsettling peace and its ambiguous morality behind him. He had what he needed to push on towards Denver. But the encounter had left him with more questions than answers, and a growing sense of the complex, often contradictory ways people found to survive, and to rule, in this broken world. His own simple cons suddenly felt very small indeed.

CHAPTER 5: THE SHADOW OF DENVER

The refined fuel from the Sanctuary of the Divine Spark was a noticeable improvement. Tweese felt it almost immediately as he guided the motorcycle away from the unsettlingly serene valley. The engine, which had been sputtering and coughing like a dying man, now purred with a smoother, more consistent rhythm. The bike responded to the throttle with a renewed vigor, the hesitation and hiccups that had plagued him for days seemingly vanished. He'd even managed to secure the promised new fuel filter from Zach, a scavenged but clean part that the quiet mechanic had meticulously installed.

Yet, the quantity of "blessed" fuel Pastor Eli had granted him was, as he'd suspected, modest. Enough to get him a good distance, certainly, but not enough to ease the gnawing anxiety about the long road still ahead. Cheyenne was a distant dream, and Denver, a looming nightmare, lay much closer. The need for a more permanent solution for fuel, and perhaps a spare filter if such a unicorn existed in this blighted world, remained a critical concern.

He rode north, the I-25 a cracked and broken spine stretching across a landscape that grew steadily more ominous. The plains here were flatter, more exposed. The ruins of pre-collapse structures appeared more frequently – not just isolated farmsteads, but the ghostly husks of what might have once been small towns or industrial parks, their metal skeletons picked clean, their concrete bones slowly crumbling back into the earth. The religious signs persisted, their white paint stark against the rust and decay, their messages of salvation and damnation becoming almost a taunting chorus in the vast emptiness. Tweese found himself scanning for them, a strange habit, wondering if the Sanctuary was the sole source, or if there were other, similar enclaves hidden in the folds of this dying world, each with its own brand of hope or subtle coercion. The air itself seemed to carry a different taint here, a faint, acrid undertone that hinted at old chemical spills and the slow rot of industrial decay, a smell that clung to the back of his throat.

As dusk began to bleed across the immense sky, casting long, distorted shadows that writhed like tormented spirits, Denver offered its first, true, unnerving welcome. It came not as a road sign, faded and bullet-riddled, but as a phenomenon that stole the breath from his chest: the "Denver Lights." Far off to the northwest, a faint, sickly yellow glow stained the darkening horizon, a diffuse luminescence that pulsed almost imperceptibly, like a diseased heart. He'd heard tales of it, of course. Travelers whispered about the Buffalo Boys and their city, how they'd somehow harnessed the power of old diesel locomotives, stolen behemoths from a forgotten age, to light up their core territory – what some called their "pleasure district," a place of rumored gambling dens and vice, all powered by the gang's iron grip. This had to be it. The light was an arrogant declaration of hoarded resources in a world starved of them, a beacon of power, but also of unimaginable danger. It spoke of a concentration of humanity, but it was a light that offered no welcome, only a warning. Tweese felt a cold knot form in his stomach, a primal unease that had nothing to do with the dropping temperature. That yellow stain on the horizon was a visual representation of everything he needed to avoid, yet it also represented the very resources he was increasingly desperate to find. He tried to pick out individual structures in the growing gloom, but it was just a jagged, broken silhouette against the dying light, punctuated by that obscene, unwavering glow.

The next morning, as the sun rose, a pale, indifferent eye in a washed-out sky, another, equally ominous sign dominated the skyline, confirming his proximity to the infamous city: the great black plume of smoke from their fuel works. He'd heard of this too, the ever-present stain that marked the Buffalo Boys' fuel production. But seeing it for the first time was different. A thick, greasy black pillar ascended relentlessly into the pale sky, a constant, unwavering column that spoke of crude industry and uncontrolled pollution. It was visible for miles, a smudge against the otherwise clear canvas, a declaration of their control over the city's vital organs. That much smoke, that constant, belching darkness, could only mean one thing: they were cracking fuel, and a lot of it. Biodiesel, rendered fats, whatever they could get their hands on, cooked down into something usable, something to power their machines and their reign. Tweese felt a knot tighten in his stomach. That smoke was where the fuel was, the lifeblood of this ravaged land. But it was also, undoubtedly, the heart of the Buffalo Boys' brutal regime, a place where, according to the darkest rumors, suffering was refined along with the oil. The plume never wavered, never thinned; it was a constant, greasy finger pointing accusingly at the heavens, a testament to the dirty, brutal power that held Denver in its grip. The distant skyline of Denver itself was a jagged wound on the horizon, a collection of broken teeth – the husks of pre-collapse skyscrapers, some leaning precariously, others just hollowed-out shells. He thought he could make out one particularly tall, dark tower, a misshapen loaf against the sky, that matched descriptions he'd heard of the "Bread Loaf," the supposed command center of the Buffalo Boys, the seat of their warlord. The sheer scale of the ruination, even from this distance, was breathtaking and appalling.

His initial plan, if it could be called such a flimsy thing born of hope and desperation, was to skirt Denver entirely. He'd spent hours hunched over his tattered map, tracing faded lines with a grimy finger, looking for any secondary roads, any old county lines or forgotten dirt tracks that might offer a bypass. The idea of taking the Iron Way jacket and the motorcycle, symbols of a hated rival, anywhere near Buffalo Boy territory was suicidal. He knew that with a certainty that chilled him to the bone. The stories of their ruthlessness were legion – summary executions, brutal public punishments, a populace kept in line by fear and starvation, tales of slave labor and every imaginable vice flourishing under their protection. But the landscape offered no easy detours. The sprawling ruins of the old suburbs formed a labyrinth of collapsed structures and impassable rubble fields, a maze of dead ends that would be treacherous even on foot, let alone on a heavy road cruiser. The map, a relic from a time of maintained infrastructure and easy travel, was proving to be a cruel liar in this new, broken world.

He spent a frustrating, sun-baked day attempting one such bypass, a faded blue line on his map that had promised to curve east around the city's sprawl, following what might have once been a railway service road. It led him into a maze of collapsed railway lines, the steel tracks twisted and torn from their sleepers like licorice sticks, and forgotten industrial ruins that loomed like the carcasses of beached whales. The ground was littered with sharp debris – shattered glass, rusted metal shards, chunks of concrete reinforced with menacing rebar fangs – and hidden pitfalls where the earth had subsided into forgotten maintenance tunnels or collapsed culverts. Twice, he had to backtrack for miles, his frustration mounting with each dead end, each impassable obstacle. The bike, despite its power, was not designed for this kind of terrain, its tires slipping on loose gravel, its suspension groaning under the strain of navigating the uneven ground.

It was in one of these desolate, forgotten corners of industrial decay, a sprawling ruin of what might have been a chemical plant, its pipes twisted into grotesque sculptures, its tanks leaking rust-colored tears, that he encountered them. He'd been picking his way through a narrow passage between two crumbling brick walls when they emerged from the shadows, silent as ghosts, blocking his path. They were five - gaunt figures draped in rags, their faces hollow-eyed and smudged with grime. They moved with a desperate, predatory quickness that spoke of long hunger and constant vigilance. Their eyes, burning with a mixture of fear and a chillingly feral hunger, fixed on him, on the bike. They were armed with crude, sharpened pipes, heavy wrenches clutched like clubs, and one carried a length of rusted chain with a heavy bolt tied to one end, a makeshift flail.

Tweese's hand instinctively went to the .45 holstered beneath his jacket. These weren't the easily cowed settlers of Walsenberg, nor the feuding farmers squabbling over water, nor even the superstitious homesteaders of Shepherd's Rest. These were creatures of the deep ruins, hardened by constant peril, their humanity stripped away by deprivation until only the raw instinct for survival remained. He'd heard Denver was brutal, that the Buffalo Boys ruled with an iron fist, but the sheer, animalistic desperation radiating from these scavengers on the city's fringe was something he hadn't fully anticipated. The stories hadn't prepared him for this. They looked like they hadn't eaten a square meal in weeks, their forms so emaciated that their tattered clothes hung loosely on their sharp-angled frames, their skin stretched taut over sharp cheekbones. There was a terrifying emptiness in their eyes, a void where hope and reason had long since died. This was the human refuse created by a regime like the Buffalo Boys, a stark contrast to the rumored decadence of their inner city. He wondered if the warlord and his cronies, in their supposedly lit and fortified strongholds, ever spared a thought for the creatures their rule spawned in the shadows.

"Bike's nice," one of them rasped, his voice like sandpaper. He was the largest, his face a mask of sores and dirt, a jagged scar bisecting one eyebrow. He took a step forward, his companions fanning out slightly, their movements coordinated, practiced. They were hemming him in. "Fuel too, I bet. And that jacket... warm."

Tweese knew that talk would be useless here. These weren't people who could be reasoned with, or bluffed with tales of the Iron Way's authority. They wouldn't care. They saw only a resource, a means to survive another day, and he was the obstacle. He was outnumbered, and they looked desperate enough to be reckless. Direct confrontation was a losing proposition.

He did the only thing he could. He revved the engine, the sudden, unexpected roar of the powerful diesel echoing explosively between the brick walls. He twisted the throttle hard, making the bike lurch forward a few feet, its front wheel rising slightly. He stood up on the pegs, making himself as large and imposing as possible, the black leather of the Iron Way jacket adding to his silhouette. He let out a guttural yell, a primal sound of aggression he hoped conveyed a savagery to match their own.

For a split second, they hesitated, their feral eyes widening slightly at the sudden noise and aggressive display. It was the opening he needed. He swerved the bike hard to the left, aiming for a narrow gap between two rusted-out chemical drums, a gap he wasn't entirely sure the bike would fit through. It was a gamble, but it was better than being dragged down and torn apart.

The handlebars scraped against one of the drums with a screech of metal on metal, sending a shower of rust flakes into the air. The bike wobbled precariously, but he held on, gunning the engine again, powering through the narrow opening. He heard shouts of anger and frustration behind him, the clatter of a dropped weapon. He didn't look back. He navigated the bike through the labyrinthine ruins, pushing it harder than he should have, the engine screaming in protest, until he finally burst out onto a relatively clear stretch of broken asphalt.

The encounter left him shaken, his heart hammering against his ribs, adrenaline a bitter taste in his mouth. Those scavengers... they were a different breed. They were what happened when people were pushed too far, when the last vestiges of civilization were stripped away.

Denver's influence, he realized, radiated outwards, poisoning the land and the people for miles around, creating a periphery of desperate, dangerous souls. The thought of facing more like them, or worse, the organized brutality of the Buffalo Boys themselves – whose cruelty he'd only heard about in whispered, fearful tales – was a cold weight in his gut. Seeing the effects firsthand, even on these outcasts, was a grim preview. The stories hadn't captured the smell of them, the hollow hunger in their eyes.

His attempt to bypass Denver had been a costly failure. He'd wasted a day, precious fuel, and had nearly lost the bike, if not his life. And the problem of his dwindling fuel supply, and the increasingly erratic performance of the motorcycle, had only grown more acute. The Sanctuary's refined fuel was almost gone, its benefits negated by the sheer strain of the off-road travel and the underlying issues with the filter he now suspected Zach hadn't fully resolved, or perhaps couldn't with the parts available. The engine was sputtering more frequently now, losing power on even slight inclines, the coughs becoming more violent. He could feel it dying beneath him, the once-powerful machine now faltering like an old man with a failing heart.

As dusk began to settle once more, casting the landscape in hues of grey and purple, he found himself back on a crumbling stretch of the I-25, the Denver Lights a more insistent, malevolent glow to the northwest, the great black plume from their refineries a thicker, more suffocating stain on the horizon. He pulled the bike over, the engine dying with a shuddering cough that sounded final. He tried the starter. Nothing. Just a click, then silence.

He was out of fuel, or so close to it that it made no difference. And the filter, he knew, was likely beyond clogged. He was stranded, with the shadow of Denver looming over him.

He sat on the useless motorcycle for a long time, the silence of the plains pressing in, punctuated by the mournful sigh of the wind through the skeletal ruins of a nearby overpass. The options paraded through his mind, each one more unpalatable than the last. He could try to push the bike, but to where? He was in the middle of nowhere, in territory that was clearly becoming more hostile. He could abandon it, try to make his way on foot, but without the bike, without the jacket, he was just another anonymous scavenger, vulnerable and alone. And the thought of abandoning the machine, this incredible, powerful machine that had become so much more than just a vehicle to him, was a bitter pill he couldn't swallow. It was his ticket, his protection, his symbol.

There was only one real option left, as much as he hated to admit it. Denver. Or at least, its outskirts. He had to get fuel. He had to get a filter. And the only place likely to have either in any quantity was the one place he desperately wanted to avoid.

The decision settled in his stomach like a stone. He would have to go in. Not as an Iron Way rider – that would be suicide. He would have to shed the persona that had served him so well, become Phillip Tweese the scavenger crow once more, a ghost slipping through the cracks.

With a heavy sigh, he dismounted. The first task was to hide the bike and the jacket. He couldn't risk taking them into the city's periphery. He scanned the desolate landscape. A short distance off the highway, half-hidden by a tangle of dead trees and overgrown bushes, was the crumbling concrete shell of what looked like it might have once been a large culvert or perhaps the entrance to an underpass that had long since collapsed. It was small, dark, and relatively concealed from the road. It would have to do.

It took him nearly an hour of back-breaking effort to wrestle the heavy motorcycle off the road, through the dense undergrowth, and into the dubious shelter of the concrete ruin. He maneuvered it as far back into the shadows as he could, then covered it as best he could with fallen branches and clumps of dried weeds. It wasn't perfect, but it might escape a casual glance.

Then came the harder part. He took off the Iron Way jacket, the heavy leather suddenly feeling like a lead weight. He folded it carefully, almost reverently, the embossed knights and roses cool beneath his fingers. This jacket had been his shield, his key, his identity for the past couple of weeks. Taking it off felt like shedding his skin, leaving him exposed and vulnerable. He tucked it into one of the saddlebags, along with most of his meager remaining provisions. He kept his knife, his binoculars, and the small pouch with a few scavenged trinkets. Critically, he also retrieved the .45 automatic and the single armor-piercing round from the other saddlebag.

He checked the pistol quickly, its familiar weight a small comfort. He then adjusted the worn leather shoulder holster, cinching it tighter than usual so it would ride high and close under his arm, less likely to print through his thin shirt. Walking into Denver openly armed was an invitation to trouble he couldn't afford; concealment was paramount now. The jacket was too conspicuous, a clear symbol of an enemy. The pistol, however, hidden but accessible, was a grim necessity for what lay ahead.

He stood for a moment in his worn shirt and trousers,

feeling strangely diminished, almost naked without the jacket's reassuring bulk, though the concealed weight of the gun offered a grim sort of reassurance. The air felt colder, the shadows deeper. He was no longer the Rider, the bringer of order, the solver of problems. He was just Phil again. Phil, the crow, picking through the leavings of a dead world, his only tools his wits, his desperation, and a single, very potent bullet.

He took one last look at the concealed motorcycle, a pang of something akin to loss tightening his chest. Then, he turned his face towards the sickly yellow glow of Denver, towards the greasy black plume from the fuel works. He took a deep breath, the air tasting of dust and distant pollution, and began to walk. Each step felt heavy, a reluctant trudge towards a fate he couldn't predict, but one he knew would be fraught with peril. The shadow of the smoke stack stretched long before him, an invitation to a hell he was about to willingly enter.

The outskirts of Denver were a sprawling, festering wound on the face of the plains. Phillip Tweese, now stripped of his Iron Way jacket and the comforting thrum of the motorcycle, felt acutely vulnerable as he picked his way through the skeletal remains of what might have once been suburbs. Ruined houses, their walls graffiti-scarred and collapsing, stood like hollow-eyed skulls, their empty windows staring out onto streets choked with debris, rusted-out vehicle husks, and the stubborn, tenacious weeds that seemed to thrive on decay. The air here was thick, carrying the distant, acrid tang of the great smoke plume he'd seen from the highway – the plume that marked the Buffalo Boys' fuel production, his reluctant destination – overlaid with the closer, more immediate stenches of uncollected refuse, stagnant water, and human desperation.

He moved like a ghost, sticking to the deepest shadows, his senses stretched taut. Every rustle of wind through broken glass, every distant shout or dog's bark, sent a jolt of adrenaline through him. He was back to being Phil the scavenger, relying on the ingrained caution and quick wits that had kept him alive for so long. The .45 automatic, nestled in its shoulder holster beneath his worn shirt, was a cold, heavy reassurance, but he knew it was a last resort, a desperate gamble against the kind of threats this city was reputed to hold.

The stories he'd heard of Denver painted it as a brutal, lawless place, ruled by the whims of the Buffalo Boys and their unseen warlord. A place of casual violence, of exploitation, where the strong preyed on the weak and life was as cheap as the dirt underfoot. He'd also heard whispers of its core, the lit and fortified areas where the gang held court, running their gambling dens and other vices. But out here, on the fringes, there was no sign of that rumored order, however corrupt. This was pure, unadulterated decay, a no-man's-land where the dispossessed and the desperate eked out a miserable existence in the ruins, like rats in a collapsed sewer. He saw furtive figures darting between crumbling buildings, their faces gaunt, their eyes holding the same feral hunger he'd seen in the scavengers who'd attacked him. He gave them a wide berth, avoiding eye contact, making himself as small and unthreatening as possible.

His goal was the source of that great black smoke plume, the place where the Buffalo Boys were rumored to crack their fuel. It was a suicidal destination, he knew. That facility, whatever it was, would be the heart of their power, heavily guarded, a place no sane outsider would willingly approach. But sanity was a luxury he couldn't afford. He needed fuel, and he needed a filter, and this was the only place in this godsforsaken territory likely to have either.

The journey towards the smoke was a slow, nerve-wracking crawl through an ever-worsening landscape of urban decay. The further he pushed into the city's ruined embrace, the more oppressive the atmosphere became. The buildings grew taller, casting deeper, more permanent shadows. The streets were more choked with rubble, forcing him into narrow, treacherous alleyways that stank of piss and old fear. He passed makeshift shantytowns, pathetic collections of lean-tos and tents fashioned from scavenged plastic sheeting and rusted corrugated iron, huddled in the lee of collapsing walls. The inhabitants, when he glimpsed them, were wraith-like figures, their faces smudged with grime, their eyes dull with a hopelessness that was almost more terrifying than the feral hunger he'd seen earlier. These were the broken ones, the people who had given up, existing in a state of numb endurance. He saw children with bellies swollen from malnutrition, their small faces old before their time, picking through piles of refuse with a practiced, joyless efficiency. The sight twisted something cold and uncomfortable in his gut.

He heard sounds, too. The distant, rhythmic thumping of what might have been a generator, the angry shouts of an argument erupting and then abruptly cut short, the mournful wail of a harmonica playing a discordant, broken tune. And always, the low, pervasive hum of the city, a sound like a million trapped insects, a sound that seemed to emanate from the very stones themselves.

As he drew closer to the industrial zone from which the smoke plume rose, the air grew thicker, the acrid tang of chemicals and unburnt fuel becoming a constant, choking presence. His eyes watered, and a metallic taste coated his tongue. The ground beneath his feet became slick in places with oily residue and unidentifiable chemical spills that shimmered with a sickly iridescence. The ruins here were different – not residential, but vast, skeletal factories, their corrugated iron walls pocked with rust and bullet holes, their towering smokestacks now silent and cold, save for the one great, active chimney that continued to vomit its black poison into the sky.

He finally reached what he judged to be the perimeter of the fuel processing facility. It was a vast, sprawling complex, surrounded by a high, formidable fence topped with wicked-looking coils of rusted barbed wire. Guard towers, crudely constructed but strategically placed, punctuated the fence line, and he could see the glint of weapons, the silhouettes of armed men, moving within them. The main gates were massive, reinforced steel, and heavily guarded by a knot of brutish-looking men in mismatched armor, their faces hard and cruel. These were Buffalo Boys, no doubt about it. Their swagger, their casual display of weaponry, the way they eyed everyone and everything with a mixture of arrogance and suspicion – it all screamed of a gang secure in its power, accustomed to unquestioned authority.

Tweese found a concealed vantage point in the shell of a bombed-out building across a wide, rubble-strewn no-man's-land from the facility's fence. From here, using his binoculars, he could observe the comings and goings, try to get a sense of their routines, their security. What he saw made his blood run cold.

The facility was a vision of hell. The air within its walls, even from this distance, seemed to shimmer with heat and toxic fumes. Great, belching furnaces roared, their flames licking at the sky. Complicated networks of pipes, many leaking steam or some noxious-looking fluid, snaked between rusted tanks and strange, clanking machinery that looked like it was on the verge of catastrophic failure. And everywhere, there were people. But these weren't the swaggering, well-armed Buffalo Boys he saw at the gates. These were... laborers. Hundreds of them, moving with a slow, shuffling gait, their bodies stooped, their clothes little more than rags. Men, women, even what looked like older children, their faces gaunt and smeared with soot and grime, toiled under the watchful eyes of brutal-looking overseers who carried heavy whips and clubs, and occasionally used them with a casual, sickening efficiency.

The laborers were engaged in back-breaking work – hauling heavy sacks of some unidentifiable raw material towards the furnaces, shoveling black, sludgy waste into overflowing pits, tending to the dangerous, poorly maintained machinery with what looked like their bare hands. The heat, even from where Tweese watched, must have been unbearable. The noise was a deafening cacophony of roaring furnaces, clanking metal, hissing steam, and the constant, brutal shouts of the overseers. The sheer scale of the operation, and the human suffering it was built upon, was overwhelming, far worse than any rumor he'd heard. This wasn't just a fuel refinery; it was a slave camp, a charnel house where human beings were consumed along with whatever raw materials they fed into the infernal machines. The stories of the Buffalo Boys' cruelty hadn't even begun to scratch the surface of this nightmare.

He watched for hours, a cold knot of disgust tightening in his stomach. His own cons, his own struggles for survival, seemed petty and insignificant in the face of this industrial-scale barbarity. He saw workers collapse from heat exhaustion or injury, only to be dragged away by the overseers with callous indifference, their places immediately taken by others.

It was as he was scanning a shadowed section of the western perimeter fence, an area partially obscured by a collapsed water tower and a tangle of rusted pipes, that he saw movement. It wasn't a guard patrol, nor the shuffling gait of a work crew. This was different. A lone figure, clad in dark, nondescript clothing that blended with the shadows, moved with a fluid, practiced stealth that spoke of experience. Tweese's breath caught. Through his binoculars, he watched, fascinated and wary, as the figure exploited a momentary gap in a guard's attention, slipped through a narrow, almost invisible break in the rusted chain-link beneath the barbed wire, and then, with the silence and grace of a cat, disappeared into the deeper shadows within the compound.

The figure was too quick, too purposeful to be one of the broken laborers. Their movements were economical, efficient, betraying a clear objective. *A thief?* Tweese wondered. *Or a spy from a rival crew?* He tracked the figure with his binoculars as it moved deeper into the refinery's guts, using the cover of machinery and piles of refuse with an expert's skill. Then, in a relatively secluded spot between two large, hissing tanks, the figure paused. Tweese watched, intrigued, as the infiltrator quickly shed the dark outer layer of clothing, revealing a bundle of what looked like tattered, filthy rags beneath. In moments, the dark garments were stashed out of sight, and the figure had donned the rags, transforming from a shadowy operative into just another indistinguishable, grime-smeared laborer. As the figure straightened and glanced around before moving to join a distant work detail, Tweese caught a brief, clearer glimpse of a lean, intelligent face, eyes that were sharp and assessing despite the attempt to mimic the downtrodden look of the other slaves. The transformation was startling in its efficiency. *Not just stealthy,* Tweese thought, a grudging respect mixing with his unease. *This one's a professional. Knows how to disappear in plain sight.* The ease with which they'd breached the perimeter and then adopted a perfect disguise was a lesson in itself. It also planted a seed of an idea – if one person could find a way in, perhaps there were other weaknesses, other blind spots he hadn't considered.

He marked the spot in his mind, the way the shadows fell from the water tower, the slight sag in the fence line. He wouldn't try it himself, not yet. His own plan was to target the dilapidated maintenance shed he'd spotted earlier, which seemed a less direct, perhaps less guarded route to potential supplies. But the knowledge that someone else was inside, someone operating with skill and a chilling level of cunning, was a strange, unsettling piece of information to file away.

Later that afternoon, as the shifts were changing and the oppressive heat seemed to reach its peak, he witnessed an act that turned the cold knot in his stomach into a burning coal of revulsion. A young worker, little more than a boy, stumbled while carrying a heavy load of what looked like slag from one of the furnaces. He dropped his burden, spilling the hot, smoking material near the feet of a particularly large, brutal-looking overseer. The overseer, a mountain of a man with a face like a clenched fist and a whip coiled in his hand, turned, his expression one of cold fury. He didn't shout. He didn't threaten. He simply uncoiled the whip and, with a practiced flick of his wrist, brought it down across the boy's back.

The sound of the lash cracking against flesh, even from this distance, was sickeningly sharp. The boy screamed, a thin, high-pitched sound of pure agony, and collapsed to the ground, writhing. The overseer watched him for a moment, his face impassive, then raised the whip again, and again, the blows falling with methodical cruelty. Other workers flinched, some turning away, but none dared intervene.

Tweese felt a surge of primitive anger, so potent it made his hands clench into fists. This was the pointless, unrestrained brutality he'd heard whispers of, made sickeningly real. A muscle in his jaw twitched, an urge to move, to do *something*, to be the man in the jacket. *The Rider would step in,* a voice in his head insisted, hot and immediate. He almost took a step forward before another, colder voice, the voice of the crow, cut through the rage. *And get yourself killed. You're not the Rider. You don't have his colors, you don't have his authority. You're just Phil.* He fought himself, the impulse to act warring with a lifetime of ingrained self-preservation. Getting involved was suicide. He was one man, looking for a part for his bike. He forced himself to look away, but the boy's screams, though faint at this distance, echoed in his mind, a corrosive counterpoint to the rhythmic clank and roar of the refinery. The image of the whip rising and falling burned itself into his memory, along with the bitter taste of his own inaction.

His primary mission, however, remained, a stubborn anchor of self-preservation. He needed a fuel filter, and he needed cleaner fuel. These weren't just immediate needs; they were crucial steps on the long road to Cheyenne, to trading the motorcycle to the Iron Way for a life where he wouldn't have to witness horrors like this, a life where he wouldn't be one misstep away from becoming one of these broken souls. That was the ultimate payoff, the dream that had pulled him this far, and it was the only thing that could justify plunging deeper into this nightmare. The sight of the refinery, the sheer, brutal efficiency of its operation, perversely confirmed that this was where those essential parts could be found. But how to get them? A direct assault was out of the question. Trying to sneak in through the main gates was equally suicidal.

He spent the rest of the dwindling daylight hours meticulously observing the facility's perimeter, forcing the boy's screams to the back of his mind, channeling his simmering anger into a cold, focused assessment of risk. He noted the shift changes of the guards, the predictable routes of the patrols, the areas around the fence line that seemed less heavily watched, perhaps due to blind spots created by collapsed structures or piles of industrial refuse. He saw a small, dilapidated maintenance shed constructed of rusted corrugated iron, tucked away near a less-guarded section of the western fence. Its door hung crookedly on one hinge, and it looked largely forgotten. *Tools might be kept there,* he thought. *Or even a spare filter, if such a thing as luck still exists in this hellhole.* It was a long shot, but it was the only potential vulnerability he could spot. The earlier infiltrator had used a different point, a more direct breach of the main fence. That was too bold for Tweese, too risky. The shed felt more his speed – less direct, more about scavenging than confrontation.

As darkness began to fall, painting the smoke-choked sky in hues of blood red and bruised purple, the Denver Lights flickered to life, casting their sickly yellow glow over the hellish landscape of the refinery. The furnaces roared, the machinery clanked, the suffering continued.

Tweese remained in his hiding place, the earlier image of the beaten boy a persistent, unwelcome guest in his thoughts. His stomach growled with hunger, but his mind was now laser-focused on the maintenance shed. He had to get closer. He had to find a way in. It was a desperate gamble, a plunge into the very heart of the Buffalo Boys' power, but the alternative – being stranded out here, his bike useless, with Denver's wolves closing in – was equally grim. He would wait for the deepest part of the night, when vigilance might be at its lowest, and then he would make his move.

CHAPTER 6: ONE BULLET, ONE SPARK

The deepest part of the night in Denver's industrial graveyard was a symphony of muted horrors. The distant, rhythmic clang of machinery from the fuel works, the occasional guttural roar of a furnace being fed, the mournful howl of some feral dog echoing through the canyons of rusted metal and crumbling brick – these were the sounds that accompanied Phillip Tweese as he began his desperate gamble. The sickly yellow glow of the Denver Lights cast an unnatural, jaundiced pall over everything, making the shadows deeper, the ruins more menacing. His stomach was a tight, aching knot of hunger and apprehension, but the image of the boy, the sound of the lash, the sheer, soul-crushing brutality he'd witnessed, had kindled a cold, hard anger that burned away some of his fear.

He moved with the practiced stealth of a seasoned scavenger, a wraith slipping through the moon-cast shadows. His target was the dilapidated maintenance shed he'd scouted earlier, tucked away near the western perimeter fence of the fuel processing facility. It was a long shot, a pathetic hope that he might find a discarded fuel filter or a forgotten jerry can of cleaner fuel amidst the refuse of the Buffalo Boys' operation. But it was the only plan he had, the only chink he'd seen in their formidable armor.

Reaching the shed was a nerve-wracking ordeal in itself. He had to cross a wide, open stretch of rubble-strewn ground, exposed to the distant, indifferent eyes of the guards in their towers. He moved in short, breathless dashes, from one meager piece of cover to the next – a rusted-out vehicle chassis, a pile of collapsed concrete, the deeper shadow of a skeletal gantry crane. Each scuff of his boot on loose gravel, each dislodged pebble, sounded like a thunderclap in the oppressive silence. The .45 under his shirt felt both a comfort and a terrible burden.

The shed, when he finally reached it, was even more decrepit up close. Its corrugated iron walls were pocked with rust holes, and the door hung precariously on a single, groaning hinge, secured by a flimsy hasp and a padlock that looked like it would yield to a well-aimed kick. He listened intently for several long minutes, straining his ears for any sound from within, but heard only the sigh of the wind through the gaps in the walls and the distant, hellish thrum of the refinery.

Taking a deep breath, he drew his sturdy camp knife. The padlock, as he'd suspected, was old and cheap. With a bit of leverage and a muffled snap of protesting metal, it gave way. He eased the door open a crack, peering into the Stygian blackness within. The air that wafted out was thick with the smell of old oil, rust, and disuse.

He slipped inside, pulling the door mostly shut behind him, leaving only a sliver open to admit a faint trace of the jaundiced Denver Lights. The interior was cluttered, chaotic. Shapes resolved themselves slowly in the gloom: workbenches littered with broken tools, piles of discarded machinery parts, empty oil drums, tangled coils of wire. He began a systematic, desperate search, his fingers probing through the grime and debris, his heart pounding with a mixture of hope and dread. He needed that filter. He needed that fuel.

His fingers brushed against something flexible and rubbery amidst a pile of rusted metal – a length of what looked like heavy-duty hose, perhaps from an old welding torch, still supple and uncracked. Nearby, he found a small, brass valve, tarnished but seemingly intact. *Not a filter,* he thought, a flicker of disappointment quickly followed by a pragmatic assessment. *But this... this could work. Bypass the clogged filter entirely. Run unfiltered for a while. It'd be rough on the engine, but it might just get me out of this damned territory, get me somewhere I can find a real fix.* He quickly stuffed the hose and valve into the small pouch at his belt. It wasn't the score he'd hoped for, but it was something. A sliver of a chance.

But that was all. No spare filters, no forgotten cans of fuel. Just more rust, more broken junk, the detritus of a brutal, uncaring operation. The shed was a bust. Despair, momentarily held at bay by his small find, began to creep in again, cold and insidious. He couldn't go back to the bike with just this. He needed fuel, actual fuel, or the hose and valve were useless. That meant going deeper.

Gritting his teeth, Tweese eased the shed door open again. The refinery pulsed with its hellish light and sound, a monstrous, living entity. He had to find where they stored the refined fuel. He slipped out of the shed, his earlier caution now sharpened by a growing desperation. He crept along the fence line, using the hulking shapes of inert machinery as cover, his eyes fixed on the massive storage tanks that dotted the complex like giant, rusted steel mushrooms. One of them, larger than the rest, was connected by a thick, insulated pipe to the clanking machinery he assumed was the final stage of the refining process. That had to be it.

He circled around, his heart pounding a frantic rhythm against his ribs, until he found himself at the base of the massive tank. It loomed over him, its curved steel wall stained with grime and rust. He ran a hand over its surface; it was thick, brutally solid plate steel, built to last in a world that hadn't. At the bottom, he found what he was looking for: a series of outflow valves. He knelt by one, trying to turn the heavy iron wheel. It was frozen solid with rust and disuse. He put all his weight into it, his muscles straining, a low grunt escaping his lips, but it wouldn't budge. He tried another. Same result. His scavenger's mind cataloged the problem: these weren't meant for casual use; they probably required a specialized wrench, a tool he didn't have.

He pulled his camp knife, trying to find purchase on the valve stem, hoping to pry something loose. The tip of his knife scraped uselessly against the hardened steel, then snapped with a sharp *tink*, the broken piece flying off into the darkness. He swore under his breath, frustration and fear a bitter taste in his mouth. As he knelt there, defeated, his eyes traced the massive curve of the tank upwards. In a small cluster on the tank wall above him, a constellation of star-shaped pockmarks marred the thick steel plate, little divots where bullets had clearly struck and failed to do more than chip the paint. Someone else had tried to bleed this beast, and had failed. A normal bullet couldn't touch this thing. His own pistol felt suddenly useless for the task.

He backed away, his mind racing. There was no easy way to get the fuel. His foray into the heart of the refinery had yielded nothing but a broken knife and a profound sense of his own inadequacy against this industrial behemoth. He had to try something else. He retreated into the more chaotic, less-guarded sections, drawn toward the organic processing area by a nauseating stench of decay and chemicals. In a dimly lit alcove, behind a bank of sputtering, clanking machinery, a stained tarpaulin lay in a heap on the floor.

What he found beneath it stopped him cold, turning the fear in his gut to ice. It was the boy. The young worker he'd seen beaten so mercilessly. His small body was still, twisted at an unnatural angle, his eyes open and staring with a dull, unseeing emptiness at the grimy, pipe-strewn ceiling. He wasn't much older than

Pip, the wide-eyed kid from Walsenberg, though this boy's gaze was now fixed in a vacant horror, a universe away from Pip's innocent curiosity. His face, even in the dim, flickering light from a nearby furnace, was a mask of dried blood and contorted pain. He wasn't just beaten; he was dead. Murdered for a spilled load of slag.

A sour heat rose in his throat. He'd seen death before, plenty of it—by starvation, by violence, by slow decay. It was a constant companion in this world. But this felt different, a violation that twisted something deep inside him. His gaze shifted from the boy's small, still form to what lay beside him, half-hidden by the tarp. A heavy-duty meat grinder, its hopper stained with something dark and viscous. Beyond it, a stack of empty, greasy barrels waited, the kind used for rendering fat. The pieces clicked into place in his mind, a sickening, logical progression. The boy. The grinder. The barrels. The fuel. His stomach convulsed, and the anger he'd suppressed earlier—the cold anger of watching the beating—returned not as a thought, but as a physical force. It was a white-hot spike driving up from his gut, flooding his veins, narrowing his vision until the only things in the world were the obscene tools of this place and the small, broken thing they were about to unmake.

The world dissolved into roaring static. All the carefully stacked justifications, the cynical rules of the scavenger crow, the voice that had told him to look away from the beating—it all shattered. The guilt from his earlier inaction was a live coal in his gut, and this obscene reality poured gasoline on it. Thoughts of fuel filters, of escape, of survival, were incinerated in a wave of pure, chemical rage. He felt his hands clench into fists, so tight his knuckles cracked and a sharp pain shot up his arm, a pain he barely registered. The only thought left, the only clear signal in the noise, was a visceral, burning need to tear this place down, to make a scar so deep it would never heal.

He didn't know how long he knelt there, staring at the boy's lifeless form, the rage a physical pressure inside his skull. But when he finally rose, his movements were calm, deliberate, imbued with a chilling sense of purpose. He still needed to get out, but now, escape was secondary. First, there would be a reckoning.

His attempt to leave the alcove undetected, however, was short-lived. As he stepped back from the horrifying scene, a figure loomed up out of the darkness – a Buffalo Boy guard, his face a mask of surprise that quickly twisted into a snarl of suspicion. "Hey! What the hell you doin' back here, skag?"

The guard's question was answered by a guttural yell as Tweese exploded into motion. There was no thought, no plan, just pure, unadulterated reaction. He surged forward, closing the distance in two quick strides, his broken camp knife held in a low, tight grip. The guard, surprised by the sudden ferocity, barely had time to raise the heavy club he carried. Tweese ignored it, ducking under the clumsy swing and driving the jagged shard of his knife into the guard's exposed forearm. The metal tore through worn fabric and flesh, and the guard screamed, a raw sound of pain and shock. The heavy club clattered to the ground as the man's hand flew open, useless. Tweese yanked the blade free and shoved the guard back, sending him stumbling into a pile of rusted barrels before the wounded man turned, clutching his arm and shouting for help as he fled.

Alarms, harsh and strident, began to blare from the guard towers. Shouts echoed through the compound. The brief, fragile illusion of stealth was shattered. Tweese knew he had seconds, maybe minutes, before he was overwhelmed. He broke into a desperate run, not towards the fence, but deeper into the labyrinth of machinery, his heart hammering a frantic rhythm against his ribs.

Heavy boots pounded on the grimy concrete behind him. "There he is! Get the skag!" a voice roared.

He rounded a massive, hissing boiler, the heat scorching his face, and found himself in a more open area, a hellish courtyard lit by the glow of the furnaces. Guards were converging from three sides, their shapes dark and menacing. And leading them, his face a mask of triumphant fury, was the overseer—the mountain of a man who had murdered the boy. He no longer carried a whip, but a heavy, spiked club, and his eyes locked onto Tweese with murderous intent.

"Nowhere to run, little man!" the overseer bellowed, his voice a gravelly roar over the din of the refinery. "Gonna enjoy this."

Tweese was cornered. His back was to a complex manifold of pipes across the courtyard from the massive, pockmarked fuel tank he'd failed to tap earlier. The gang of thugs fanned out, cutting off any escape, their expressions a mixture of bloodlust and cruel amusement. The overseer took a step forward, hefting his club.

The world seemed to slow down. The roar of the furnaces, the shouts of the guards, it all faded into a low hum. All Tweese could see was the overseer's leering face, the face of the man who had discarded a child like garbage. The rage inside him coalesced into a single point of cold, clear purpose. He yanked the .45 from its holster. The movement was fluid, born of pure instinct.

The overseer laughed, a short, brutal bark. "Gonna shoot me, skag? With that peashooter? Go on. Try."

Tweese raised the pistol, the heavy steel a steady weight in his hand. He leveled the barrel, sighting down its length, his entire world narrowing to the front sight and the sneering face beyond it. The guards flanking the overseer hesitated, their own weapons half-raised, curious to see the show. He was outmanned, outgunned, and this was a fool's last stand. He let his aim center on the space between the overseer's eyes, a silent promise of retribution.

He squeezed the trigger.

The .45 bucked in his hand, its roar deafening even amidst the din of the refinery. For a heart-stopping moment, nothing happened. The overseer, his sneer frozen on his face, didn't fall. A couple of the guards chuckled, thinking Tweese had missed, that his one desperate act of defiance had been a pathetic failure. The overseer's eyes widened in a look of triumphant mockery.

Then, a high-pitched, metallic *ping* echoed from *behind* the overseer, impossibly sharp, followed by a sound like the gates of hell being torn open.

The world erupted. A dome of pure white light bloomed outwards, vaporizing the night, followed an instant later by a concussive blast that felt less like sound and more like a physical blow from a giant's fist. It threw him off his feet, slamming him hard against the grimy concrete. The ground beneath him heaved and bucked like a frightened horse. The air, sucked from his lungs, was replaced by the shriek of tearing metal and a deep, guttural roar that seemed to shake the very foundations of the world. He felt a searing heat wash over him, scalding his exposed skin, and the acrid smell of burning fuel and vaporized chemicals filled his lungs, choking him.

Through ringing ears and swimming vision, he pushed himself up, dazed. The storage tank he'd aimed near was gone, replaced by a twisted, blazing ruin, spewing a geyser of liquid fire hundreds of feet into the night sky. Secondary explosions began to rip through the complex as the fire spread with terrifying speed, a chain reaction of destruction. A smaller tank went up with a deep *WUMP*, sending a fireball spiraling into the smoke-choked heavens. Pipes burst, spraying flaming fuel across the compound.

Chaos reigned. Alarms shrieked, a futile scream drowned out by the roar of the inferno. Figures ran blindly through the smoke and fire, some burning, their bodies living torches, their screams swallowed by the noise. The Denver Lights flickered and died as power lines snapped and generators failed, plunging the surrounding area into a deeper darkness, making the conflagration seem even brighter, more terrible.

Tweese knew this was his only chance. He scrambled to his feet, his body aching, his ears ringing, but a wild, almost exultant energy coursing through him. He'd done it. He'd struck a blow. He'd lit a spark.

He began to run, not towards the main gate – that would be a death trap – but towards the western perimeter, towards the section of fence where he'd seen the other infiltrator slip through earlier. It was a desperate hope, a long shot, but it was the only path that offered even a sliver of a chance.

As he stumbled through the smoke and chaos, dodging falling debris and panicked figures, he saw a familiar lean shape detach itself from the pandemonium near the compromised fence line. It was the infiltrator he'd seen earlier, the one who had changed into slave rags. The figure paused for a fraction of a second, their sharp eyes meeting Tweese's across the fiery, smoke-filled expanse in a fleeting, assessing glance. Then, the infiltrator turned and, with that same fluid, practiced grace, slipped through the breach in the fence and vanished into the darkness beyond.

Tweese didn't hesitate. He followed, his lungs burning, his heart pounding. He squeezed through the narrow gap, the barbs tearing at his clothes, and found himself outside the inferno, back in the relative quiet of the ruined industrial zone. He didn't look back. He just ran, fueled by adrenaline and the horrifying, exhilarating knowledge of what he had done.

He had come to Denver seeking a fuel filter. He was leaving behind a conflagration. He had no idea if he'd gotten what he came for, no idea if he'd even survive the night. But as he fled into the darkness, the roar of the burning refinery a fading echo behind him, he knew this wasn't something Phil the crow, the detached scavenger, would ever have done. He had acted without thinking, without the familiar calculations of risk and reward.

CHAPTER 7:
JOHNSTON'S CORNER

The darkness of the plains outside Denver was a suffocating blanket, but for Phillip Tweese, it was a sanctuary. He ran, his lungs burning, every muscle screaming in protest, the roar of the burning refinery a fading but still terrifying symphony at his back. The acrid smell of chemicals and burning fuel clung to him, a foul perfume he suspected would take days to wash away, if he ever found enough clean water to try. His ears rang from the concussive force of the explosion, and his vision still swam with the ghost-images of fire and twisted metal.

He'd done it. He'd actually done it. He'd aimed that single, precious armor-piercing round not at the man, but at the guts of their operation, and had torn a hole in their world. The thought brought a grim, almost exultant satisfaction, quickly chased by a cold wave of terror at the magnitude of what he'd unleashed. He was a con man, a scavenger, not a saboteur who crippled vital infrastructure of a major gang. Or at least, he hadn't been.

The adrenaline that had fueled his desperate flight began to ebb, leaving behind a bone-deep weariness and a throbbing ache in every limb. He'd been thrown hard by the blast, and his shoulder screamed where he'd landed on it. He stumbled on, putting as much distance as possible between himself and the hell he'd ignited. Behind him, the steady, sickly yellow glow of the Denver Lights was now rivaled by the chaotic, leaping orange of the inferno, a new and terrible dawn rising from the earth to challenge the old. The single, greasy pillar of smoke that had long defined the horizon was gone, replaced by a churning, chaotic cloud that boiled into the heavens.

He didn't know if the lean infiltrator he'd followed through the fence had made it clear, or even noticed him tag along. The figure had vanished into the night as quickly and silently as they'd appeared, another ghost in the ruins. Tweese was alone again, with the consequences of his actions chasing him like hounds.

Did he get what he came for? In the chaos of the explosion and escape, the thought of a fuel filter or a can of fuel had been obliterated by the more pressing need to simply survive. He clutched the small pouch at his belt; the hose and valve he'd found in the shed were still there. Meager winnings for such a high-stakes gamble, and useless without fuel.

It took what felt like an eternity, stumbling through the pre-dawn gloom, before he dared to circle back towards the I-25 and the place where he'd hidden the motorcycle. Every shadow seemed to hold a Buffalo Boy, every gust of wind carried the imagined sound of pursuit. His heart hammered against his ribs, a frantic drumbeat counting down the moments until discovery.

He found the collapsed culvert just as the first, pale fingers of dawn were stretching across the eastern sky, painting the undersides of the clouds in hues of grey and bruised purple. With trembling hands, he pulled away the branches and weeds he'd used for camouflage. The motorcycle was there, untouched, its dark form a solid, reassuring presence in the dim light. Relief, so potent it almost buckled his knees, washed over him. It was still his.

He quickly retrieved the Iron Way jacket from the saddlebag. The heavy leather felt different now, not just a costume, but something more. He'd acted, not as a grifter playing a part, but as something else, something closer to the man the jacket represented. The thought was unsettling, foreign, yet undeniable. He shrugged it on, the familiar weight a strange comfort. He checked the .45, re-holstering it under the jacket.

The immediate problem was fuel. The tank was dry. He had the hose and valve, but no way to bypass the filter without something to feed the engine. He scanned the desolate surroundings, his scavenger's eyes searching for any sign of opportunity. It was a long shot, but sometimes the wasteland offered unexpected gifts to those desperate enough to look. His gaze settled on a shape half-buried in a ditch not far from the culvert: a rusted-out hulk of an old agricultural machine, a combine or something similar. These things often had small auxiliary fuel tanks, sometimes overlooked by other scavengers.

Getting to the tank was a battle. The bolts holding its retaining straps were fused with a century of rust, their hexagonal heads rounded into smooth, mocking circles. He put his wrench on one, the metal teeth slipping uselessly. He tried again, bracing his foot against the combine's chassis, putting every ounce of his weight into it. Sweat dripped into his eyes, and a sharp, firework-like pain exploded in his slashed forearm, making him hiss through his teeth. The bolt didn't move. He found a hefty rock and began to hammer the end of the wrench, the sharp clang of metal on metal echoing across the quiet plains. Every strike sent fresh waves of agony up his arm, but it also sent a fresh wave of panic through him. The noise seemed impossibly loud. He kept pausing, his heart hammering, scanning the horizon for movement, certain that a Buffalo Boy patrol would crest the nearest rise, drawn by the sound. He thought he saw a flicker of motion at the edge of his vision and dropped flat, his breath catching in his throat, but it was only a tumbleweed, dancing in the morning breeze.

Finally, with a last, desperate shriek of tortured metal, the first bolt gave way. The second was just as stubborn. The fuel lines were brittle, cracking under the slightest pressure, forcing him to work with a surgeon's delicacy that felt absurd given the brute force he'd just employed. At last, after what felt like another precious hour of nerve-shredding noise and pained effort, the small, dented auxiliary tank came free, sloshing with the promise of movement. It held a gallon, maybe two, of sludgy, questionable diesel. It wasn't much, and it was probably as dirty as the fat-fuel he'd been using, but it was something. He almost laughed then, a harsh, dry sound that scraped his raw throat. All that fire and brimstone back in Denver, the sheer terror and the blood, and here was a puddle of salvation sitting right under his nose the whole damned time. *"Praise the Spark,"* he thought, the words a bitter, metallic taste in his mouth, echoing Pastor Eli's smooth platitudes. *Or maybe just praise dumb luck and the universe's rotten sense of humor.*

He poured the fuel into his canteen, a slow, messy process that left his hands stinking of old diesel. He looked at the motorcycle's engine, then at the hose and valve in his pouch. He could rig the bypass now. It would take time, more tinkering, more risk of being discovered. He looked at the sludgy, particle-filled liquid in his canteen. This wasn't the clean fuel from the Sanctuary. Running this stuff directly into the engine, unfiltered, was a good way to seize it up for good. His current filter was clogged, sure, but it might still catch the worst of this crap. It was a choice between two bad options: stay here and risk a patrol stumbling upon him while he performed delicate surgery, or get moving with what he had and hope the choked filter did its job just long enough. It wasn't a choice at all. He had to get away from Denver.

With the small amount of salvaged diesel in the motorcycle's tank, the engine coughed to life, sputtering and protesting, but it ran. The sound was a prayer answered. He didn't waste a moment, guiding the bike back onto the broken ribbon of the I-25, heading north, away from the pillar of smoke that still stained the southern horizon, a testament to his night's work.

The ride north was a grim, nerve-wracking affair. Tweese pushed the bike, and himself, relentlessly. Every distant plume of dust, every unexpected sound, sent his heart racing, his hand instinctively going to the .45, though he knew it was now just an empty weight. He imagined Buffalo Boy patrols fanning out, hunting for the saboteur who had crippled their refinery. He was more haunted now, less the glib opportunist he'd been just days ago. The images from the refinery – the endless toil, the casual cruelty, the dead boy, the meat grinder – were burned into his mind, a gallery of horrors that replayed with every mile. He felt changed, scoured raw by what he'd seen and done. The "heroic" acts he'd performed in the smaller settlements felt like child's play compared to the inferno he'd unleashed in Denver. That had been real, visceral, a direct confrontation with an evil so profound it had demanded an equally profound response.

The urban sprawl of Denver's northern outskirts gave way slowly. For miles, the highway was flanked by the decaying husks of what must have been endless suburbs – Aurora, Commerce City, Thornton – names as dead as the ruins that bore them, now just an undifferentiated mass of decay. He passed a bizarre, ghostly landmark: a sprawling, sun-bleached ruin of a pre-collapse amusement park. A giant, faded red rock arch dominated the landscape, a crude mockery of something he'd once seen on a peeling postcard scavenged from a dead traveler's pack—a picture of a place called Arches. It was clearly the centerpiece of what had been an elaborate miniature golf course, its once-green carpets now patchy and brown, its whimsical obstacles – castles, windmills, dinosaurs – crumbling and vandalized. Beside it, two massive fiberglass tubes, once brightly colored but now faded to pastel chalk, twisted around each other in a double helix, the skeletal remains of water slides, their pools long since cracked and filled with debris. A faded sign, barely legible, proclaimed "ARCHES OF FUN - GOLF - KARTS - SLIDES!" The sheer, pointless frivolity of it, juxtaposed with the grim realities of the world he now inhabited, and the fresh horror of Denver, struck Tweese as profoundly absurd. He imagined children laughing here once, a lifetime ago, and the thought was like a shard of glass in his gut.

Further north, the character of the I-25 began to change. He noticed stretches where the worst of the debris seemed to have been pushed to the sides, the potholes crudely filled with packed earth and gravel. It wasn't proper maintenance, not by Before Times standards, but it was an effort. He even saw a few faded, stenciled symbols on concrete barriers – a stylized cog or gear, something he vaguely associated with whispered tales of the Iron Way's road-clearing crews. It gave him a flicker of something that wasn't quite hope, but perhaps a lessening of immediate dread. If the Iron Way truly patrolled this far south, maybe the worst of the lawless chaos was behind him.

Then, disaster. Or at least, a major inconvenience. An entire overpass, one of the massive concrete spans that had once carried lesser roads over the interstate, had collapsed, its guts spilling onto the highway below in a mountain of twisted rebar and shattered concrete. It completely blocked both northbound lanes. There was no way through. Cursing his luck, Tweese was forced to backtrack and find a crumbling service road that paralleled the I-25, hoping it would eventually lead him around the obstruction.

The detour took him through a landscape of forgotten fields, now overgrown with thorny scrub, and past the skeletal remains of isolated farmhouses. Navigating a particularly rough patch of what had once been a county road, his attention was caught by an old, red-brick firehouse, surprisingly intact despite its broken windows and sagging roof. And in the gaping bay where a fire engine might once have stood, a small herd of wild horses had taken shelter from the midday sun. They were lean, shaggy beasts, their coats dusty, but their eyes were bright and alert. They watched him pass, their ears swiveling, but made no move to flee. For a moment, Tweese just stared, a strange sense of peace washing over him. He didn't linger, not wanting to disturb them, but the image stayed with him.

Back on the I-25, north of the collapse, the signs of Iron Way influence became slightly more pronounced. He passed a few small, fortified settlements – little more than a cluster of buildings surrounded by high, scrap-metal walls and watchtowers – nestled a short distance from the highway. They looked more organized, more defensible than the desperate hovels he'd seen further south, closer to Denver. Yet, their very defensiveness, the clear effort put into their fortifications, suggested that even here, under the supposed umbrella of Iron Way control, life was far from secure. It planted a small seed of doubt about the all-encompassing protection he'd imagined the gang provided.

As the afternoon wore on, the highway began to dip into a series of shallow valleys. The air grew cooler, and a strange, localized mist clung to the low-lying areas, even though the sky above was clear. He passed a faded sign, its letters barely legible: "EERIE - NEXT EXIT." The name felt apt. The fog swirled around the ruins of the small town, half-obscuring the buildings, making them look like ghostly apparitions. A profound silence hung in the air, disturbed only by the drip of condensation from unseen structures and the nervous thrum of his own engine. He pushed the bike a little faster, eager to be out of the unsettling miasma.

The sputtering engine forced a slower pace as he climbed out of the eerie lowlands, and the sun was beginning to dip towards the jagged peaks of the distant mountains when he passed a series of faded, bullet-scarred green signs. Most of the lettering was illegible, but he could make out the fragmented name "L...GM...NT". Longmont, he guessed, or what was left of it. The ruins here were more extensive than many he'd passed, a sprawling ghost town of collapsed strip malls and hollowed-out suburban homes, their emptiness told a story of the long decline. As he cleared the last of Longmont's skeletal remains, the plains opening up again, his gaze caught on a structure in the distance: a massive, old-world billboard, its original vibrant colors faded to pale ghosts, its metal structure pocked with rust and bullet holes. Much of the original advertisement – something about "World Famous Cinnamon Rolls" and "Best Gas on I-25!" – was obscured by a newer, cruder layer of paint. Stark white letters, bold against the peeling pastels of the old ad, now proclaimed: "JOHNSTON'S CORNER - 5 MILES. TRADE. REFUEL. ALL WELCOME (NO TROUBLE)." Beneath the words was a rough but recognizable drawing of a steaming coffee cup next to a fuel can. Hope, a fragile commodity, flickered anew.

A few miles later, Johnston's Corner itself came into view. It was a fortress of stacked and welded shipping containers, forming a high, defensible perimeter. Smoke curled from a few stovepipe chimneys, and he could see figures moving about on catwalks that connected the upper levels. The repurposed billboard hadn't lied; it looked like an island of rough-hewn order in a sea of chaos, a vital, relatively neutral trading hub, according to the whispers he'd heard.

He approached cautiously, the motorcycle's engine coughing more insistently now. He could see armed guards at the gate, their expressions watchful but not overtly hostile. This place had a reputation for being a neutral zone, where even rival factions could come to trade, under the watchful eye of its proprietor. He hoped that reputation was accurate. He needed fuel, desperately. He needed a safe place to rest, to think, to try and make sense of the whirlwind he'd just passed through.

As he neared the gate, one of the guards, a burly man with a shotgun resting in the crook of his arm, raised a hand. "Hold up there, Rider. State your business."

Tweese cut the engine, the silence that followed amplifying the thumping of his own heart. He pushed up his goggles, his face grimy, his eyes bloodshot and weary. He was still wearing the

Iron Way jacket. He felt he'd earned the right to it now, not through pretense, but through action. "Name's Phil," he said, his voice raspy. "Bike's running on fumes and hope. Looking for fuel, maybe some parts. Saw your sign back down the road. Heard this was a place a man could trade."

The guard looked him over, his gaze lingering on the jacket, then on the battered state of the motorcycle. "Iron Way, huh? Seen a few of your kind passin' through. Johnston's is open for trade, long as you keep the peace. Bill runs a tight ship." He gestured towards the gate. "Head on in. Park the bike by the workshops. Someone'll see to ya."

Tweese nodded, relief washing over him. He nudged the bike forward, the engine sputtering back to life with a reluctant cough. The gate creaked open, and he rode into the compound.

The interior of Johnston's Corner was a bustling, chaotic hive of activity. The courtyard, formed by the towering walls of shipping containers, was a fragile island of commerce in a sea of chaos. Makeshift stalls and rough-hewn tables piled with goods were crowded with a motley assortment of travelers – scavengers, settlers, traders, even a few hard-bitten individuals who looked like they might belong to one gang or another. The air was thick with the smell of woodsmoke, cooking food, dust, and human bodies. Tensions, he could sense, were always simmering beneath the surface here, given the loose mix of factions.

He spotted a young man, maybe sixteen or seventeen, leaning against a stack of crates, idly whittling a piece of wood with a sharp knife. He was skinny and wiry, with an unkempt poof of dark hair tied back from a face that was all sharp angles and keen, observant eyes. Those eyes missed nothing, sweeping over Tweese and his motorcycle with a quick, assessing glance that seemed to take in every detail. The kid looked street-smart, like he'd grown up navigating the complex currents of a place like this.

Tweese parked the bike where the guard had indicated, near a collection of open-fronted containers that seemed to serve as workshops. The engine died with a final, wheezing gasp. He was running on empty.

Before he could even dismount, an older man emerged from what looked like the main office – another container, this one with a proper door and a couple of grimy windows. He was weathered, his face a roadmap of hard lines, but his eyes held a spark of weary intelligence. He carried a shotgun easily, like an extension of his own arm, its presence a clear statement of authority. This had to be Bill.

"Welcome to Johnston's Corner, Rider," Bill said, his voice calm but firm. "Looks like you've had a rough trip." His gaze took in the jacket, the bike, and Tweese's exhausted state. "What can we do for you?"

Tweese felt a measure of the tension ease from his shoulders. This place, despite its rough edges, felt…safer than anywhere he'd been since leaving the Sanctuary. He was still on edge, the inferno of Denver still burning in his memory, but here, at least, he might find a moment's respite. And fuel. Definitely fuel. The first step towards Cheyenne, and the life he was now more desperate than ever to reach.

The shotgun Bill carried looked like it had seen as many hard miles as the man himself. It was an old pump-action, its wooden stock scarred and dark with oil, its metal parts worn to a dull grey patina. But there was no doubt it was functional, and Bill handled it with an easy familiarity that spoke of long practice. His eyes, though, were the most arresting thing about him. They were a pale, washed-out blue, set deep in a face carved by sun and wind and worry, and they held a shrewd, assessing quality that missed little. They flicked over Tweese, taking in the grime, the exhaustion, the Iron Way jacket that felt suddenly heavy and conspicuous, and the battered state of the motorcycle.

"Rough trip, you say?" Bill's voice was calm, a gravelly baritone that held no immediate judgment, only a weary sort of acknowledgment. "Most trips are, these days. Especially coming up from the south. What can Johnston's Corner do for a Rider in need?"

Tweese swung a leg over the motorcycle, his muscles screaming in protest. The adrenaline from the escape and the desperate ride north had long since worn off, leaving behind a bone-deep fatigue and a collection of aches that promised to make themselves known for days. "Fuel, mostly," he said, his voice still raspy. "This old girl's running on prayers and bad intentions right now." He patted the motorcycle's tank. "And a filter, if such a thing exists in this part of the world. Mine's choked near to death." He paused, then added, "Could use a place to rest a bit, too. Maybe some information on the road north to Cheyenne."

Bill nodded slowly, his gaze unwavering. "Fuel we got, of various grades. Filters are scarcer than hen's teeth, but we might have something that can be made to fit. Tuba!" He raised his voice slightly, and the skinny young man Tweese had noticed earlier, the one whittling by the crates, looked up, his keen eyes flicking towards them. "Show this Rider where he can bunk down for a bit. And see if you can scrounge him some cleaner rags and water. Looks like he's worn most of Denver home with him."

The young man – Tuba – pushed himself off the crates and sauntered over, his movements loose-limbed and economical. He had a wiry strength to him, and his eyes, dark and intelligent, took in Tweese with an unnervingly direct and appraising stare. There was no fear there, Tweese noted, nor any particular deference to the Iron Way jacket. Just a cool, watchful curiosity. This wasn't like the awestruck settlers further south. This kid had seen his share of hard cases, Tweese figured.

"This way, Rider," Tuba said, his voice surprisingly deep for his lean frame. He gestured with the knife he'd been whittling with – a well-made, practical-looking blade – towards a row of containers that seemed to have been converted into living quarters.

"Appreciate it," Tweese said, giving Bill a nod. "We can talk trade for the fuel and parts when I've… settled in."

"No hurry," Bill replied, his expression unreadable. The Corner ain't going nowhere. Get yourself sorted. We'll talk later." He turned and headed back towards the office container, the shotgun still held loosely in his hand.

Tuba led Tweese to a small, surprisingly clean container fitted with a couple of rough cots and a small, battered table. It was spartan, but it was shelter, and it felt blessedly secure after the horrors of the refinery and the nerve-wracking flight. "Water's in the bucket yonder," Tuba said, pointing. "Rags are on the cot. Latrine's out back, past the workshops. Bill'll likely be in the main cafe container when you're ready to talk business. Or I can fetch him."

"This'll do fine," Tweese said. "Thanks… Tuba, was it?"

The young man nodded, his eyes still holding that unnervingly sharp focus. "Anything else, Rider?"

Tweese hesitated. He was exhausted, filthy, and his mind was still reeling from the events in Denver. But he needed to maintain the persona, at least for now. "Just the fuel and the filter for the bike. And maybe a hot meal, if there's one to be had that doesn't taste like despair."

A flicker of something – amusement? understanding? – crossed Tuba's face. "Bill's a fair cook, for an old grifter. Better than most. I'll let him know you're looking for him." With another nod, Tuba was gone, moving with that same quiet, efficient grace.

Left alone, Tweese sank onto one of the cots, the springs groaning in protest. He stripped off the grimy layers of his own clothes, wincing as fabric pulled at the half-healed slash on his arm from the guard in the refinery shed. He splashed water on his face and neck, scrubbing away the worst of the soot and grime. The water was cool, and it felt like a benediction.

As he cleaned himself up, his mind replayed the inferno. The dead boy. The meat grinder. The roar of the explosion. He felt a grim satisfaction at the destruction he'd caused, a feeling that was quickly followed by a cold wave of unease. He'd hurt people, maybe killed some, and unleashed chaos on a scale he'd never imagined. He looked at his hands, turning them over. They were steady, but they felt like they belonged to a stranger. These were the hands that had just pulled that trigger. He tried to summon the old calculus of the crow, the simple math of risk versus reward that had kept him alive for so long. But the numbers wouldn't add up. The image of the boy's empty eyes kept getting in the way, a debt that couldn't be factored into any equation. He'd taken off the Rider's jacket before entering Denver, shedding the skin to become the scavenger again. But the disguise had been for others. He realized now that the man who had set a city on fire was the same man who had worn the jacket all along.

Later, feeling marginally more human, he sought out Bill in the main cafe container. It was a long, narrow space, fitted with a rough counter, a few mismatched tables and chairs, and the pervasive smell of boiled coffee and frying fat. A handful of grim-looking travelers were hunched over mugs or plates of food, their conversations low and guarded. Bill was behind the counter, wiping it down with a rag, his shotgun leaning within easy reach.

"Feeling better, Rider?" Bill asked, his eyes assessing.

"Some," Tweese admitted. "Ready to talk about that fuel. And the filter."

They haggled for a while, a familiar dance of offer and counter-offer that Tweese, despite his exhaustion, found almost comforting in its normalcy. Bill was a shrewd trader, but fair. He had a small stock of refined biodiesel – "Good stuff, not that rendered crap that'll choke your lines in a week," he claimed – and after much searching through a pile of scavenged parts, Tuba, who had reappeared silently at some point, produced a fuel filter that looked like it might fit, or could be adapted with the hose and valve Tweese had salvaged. The price was steep – most of the trinkets Tweese had hoarded, plus a promise of a day's labor around the compound if the repairs took longer than expected. Tweese agreed. He needed the bike running, and running clean.

As Tuba set to work on the motorcycle in one of the workshop containers, his movements deft and surprisingly skilled for someone so young, Tweese found himself observing life at Johnston's Corner. It was a microcosm of the wasteland, a fragile island of commerce in a sea of chaos. Traders came and went, their faces hard, their eyes wary. Scavengers bartered meager finds for a mouthful of food or a few rounds of ammunition. Families, their faces etched with the hardship of the road, huddled together, seeking a moment's respite before pushing on. And through it all, Bill moved with a quiet authority, his presence a constant, a guarantor of the fragile peace.

A pair of figures near the main gate cut through the courtyard's chaotic noise without raising their voices. They were an island of quiet authority in a sea of desperation. Both wore the black leather of the Way, but where Tweese's was an affectation, theirs was a uniform worn with the unthinking ease of long habit. The older one was built like a blacksmith's anvil, barrel-chested with a thick salt-and-pepper beard that couldn't hide the hard lines etched around his mouth. His leathers were scuffed at the knees and elbows, worn thin in the way that only comes from thousands of miles and countless seasons on the road, yet they were meticulously cared for. He stood with a stillness that was more intimidating than any overt threat, his eyes, pale and cold as river stones, missing nothing. The younger one beside him was a coiled spring of restless energy. Barely out of his teens, his leathers were newer, the black dye still deep and unfaded. He shifted his weight from foot to foot, his hand repeatedly brushing the hilt of a knife at his belt, his gaze flicking around the courtyard with a hungry, proprietary arrogance that hadn't quite settled into the older man's cold confidence. On the shoulder of each jacket was a small, stitched patch of a stylized cog. Their motorcycles, parked nearby, were not merely transports but tools of their trade—powerful, functional, and stripped of anything but purpose.

Real Iron Way.

A jolt of anxiety, cold and sharp, shot through Tweese. His throat felt tight. He could feel the blood thrumming in his ears, a sudden, panicked drumbeat. *This is it,* he thought, his mind racing. *The end of the line.* His dream of trading the bike for a peaceful plot of land felt like a child's fantasy. The reality was two hard-looking men who would see him not as a peer, but as a thief wearing a dead man's clothes. The reputation he'd so carefully borrowed was about to come due, with an interest rate he couldn't possibly pay.

He tried to appear casual, turning away, busying himself with checking the straps on his (mostly empty) saddlebags. But he could feel their presence, a weight in the air. He was acutely aware of the jacket on his back, the embossed knights and roses that suddenly felt like a brand.

Tuba, emerging from under the bike, wiped grease from his hands on a rag. He followed Tweese's gaze to the two Iron Way riders. "Them's Aron and Jack-Jack," Tuba said, his voice low. "Regulars, mostly. Though Aron ain't been this far south in years, from what he was saying to Bill earlier. Heading down to check on some new toll station, I heard."

The names, casually dropped by Tuba, landed like small stones in Tweese's gut. Hearing them named, hearing they were *regulars* here, brought a fresh wave of unease. It meant they were known quantities, recognized figures. It hadn't fully occurred to him that the closer he got to Iron Way territory, the more likely he was to encounter people who actually *knew* members of the gang, people who wouldn't be so easily fooled by a jacket and a story. A kid like Tuba, sharp as he was, might idly mention to these regulars that another "Rider" had passed through, and any discrepancy, any odd detail, could unravel his entire charade. His stomach tightened. This was it. The real deal. He had to be careful. One wrong word, one misplaced gesture, and his whole charade could come crashing down.

"They seem... professional," Tweese said, trying to keep his voice neutral.

Tuba shrugged, his eyes still on the riders, then flicking back to Tweese with that unnervingly perceptive gaze. "They get the job done. Keep some of the roads clearer than they'd be otherwise. Charge a steep price for it, though, one way or another." There was no admiration in his voice, only a flat statement of fact. "They don't talk much, not to folks like us. All business." He paused, then looked directly at Tweese, his head tilted slightly. "You're different from them, Rider."

Tweese felt a prickle of alarm. "Different? How so?"

"More... talkative, for one," Tuba said, a faint, almost challenging glint in his eye. "And that jacket... it's a nice piece of leather. Old style. Haven't seen one with that kind of fancy stitching on an Iron Way man before. Most of theirs are plain, or just got the cog."

CHAPTER 8: THE RIDER'S REFLECTION

The thin light of dawn had barely begun to creep over the stacked container walls of Johnston's Corner when Tweese found himself stirring. Sleep had been a fitful, shallow thing, punctuated by jarring images of fire, the vacant stare of the dead boy, and the unnervingly perceptive gaze of young Tuba. The kid's words from the previous day – "You're different from them, Rider" – had echoed in his mind, a persistent, disquieting counterpoint to the muted sounds of the trading post settling down for the night. The metallic tang of blood and burnt fuel still seemed to coat the back of his throat, a phantom taste of Denver's horrors.

He rose from the cot, his body stiff and aching, each movement a reminder of his desperate flight. The relative safety of Johnston's Corner, which had felt like a godsend upon his arrival, now seemed precarious, almost claustrophobic. Aron and Jack-Jack, the real Iron Way riders, were here. Their presence was a constant, unspoken threat, a palpable weight in the dusty air. He'd seen them from a distance in the common area the previous evening, their easy confidence, the way other traders gave them a wide berth, all speaking of an established authority he could only mimic. Every casual glance in their direction, every snippet of their gruff conversation he inadvertently overheard as he'd choked down his meal, sent a fresh jolt of anxiety through him. He felt like a man walking a tightrope over a pit of vipers, the Iron Way jacket a heavy, conspicuous burden rather than a shield. Its familiar weight, once a source of borrowed confidence, now felt like a leaden shroud.

He spent the early morning trying to make himself scarce, keeping to the periphery of the bustling courtyard. Johnston's Corner was already coming alive. The smells of woodsmoke from cookfires, brewing chicory, and the sharp tang of animal dung mingled in the cool air. Traders were unlashing goods from pack animals, their voices low and businesslike. The clang of a hammer on metal echoed from one of the workshop containers. Tweese kept his head down, his eyes constantly scanning for the two riders, his senses on high alert. He needed to get the motorcycle fully operational and then get out, before his luck, which had been stretched perilously thin, finally snapped. The thought of confronting Aron, of trying to explain his possession of the bike, was unthinkable. The idealized image he'd begun to build of the Iron Way – noble protectors, bringers of order – was already starting to crack under the weight of Tuba's casual observations and his own dawning, sickening unease. They were just another gang, weren't they? More organized, perhaps, with a better public image in some quarters, but a gang nonetheless, with a gang's brutal intolerance for those who crossed them.

He found Tuba near the workshops, where the young man was already hunched over the motorcycle's engine, his movements economical and surprisingly assured for someone his age. The kid had a knack for mechanics, that much was clear. The new filter, scavenged from Bill's eclectic collection of parts, was in place, and Tuba was now meticulously checking the fuel lines, his brow furrowed in concentration. A smear of grease already adorned one sharp cheekbone.

"Morning, Rider," Tuba said, not looking up from his work, his voice low, almost casual, but Tweese detected an undercurrent, a knowingness that set his teeth on edge. "She'll be ready to roll in an hour or so. Had to clean out some more gunk from the line. That diesel you found near Denver was pretty rough stuff. Surprised it got you this far." He finally glanced up, his eyes sharp. "You were lucky to find any at all, I guess."

"Appreciate the help," Tweese said, trying to sound nonchalant. He leaned against a stack of old tires, the rubber smelling faintly of decay and ozone. He feigned an interest in Tuba's work, watching the young man's nimble fingers, but his mind was racing. He needed to gauge how much the kid suspected. He'd seen a look like the one Tuba gave him yesterday a handful of times before, and it always preceded trouble. It was the look a mark gets just before they stop believing the story and start looking for the lie, a subtle shift from passive acceptance to sharp, focused assessment. It was a look that meant the game was about to change.

Tuba tightened a clamp with a decisive twist of a wrench, then finally looked up, his dark eyes meeting Tweese's with that same unnerving directness. "Bill says you're heading for Cheyenne. To meet up with your brothers in the Way." It wasn't a question; it was a statement, flat and uninflected.

"That's the plan," Tweese confirmed, his voice carefully neutral, hoping it didn't betray the sudden tightness in his chest.

Tuba nodded slowly, his gaze never leaving Tweese's face. He wiped his greasy hands on an equally greasy rag. "Aron and Jack-Jack, they're heading north too, eventually. After they check on that new toll station down south. Might be you'll cross paths with them again." He paused, letting the implication hang in the air like the dust motes dancing in the thin shafts of morning light piercing the workshop's gloom. "Or maybe they'll hear about you before then."

Tweese felt a cold knot tighten in his stomach. His mouth went dry. "Hear about me?" he managed, his voice sounding distant to his own ears.

"Word travels," Tuba said, his voice still quiet, almost conversational, yet carrying the weight of a hammer blow. "Especially when things blow up down Denver way. Big fire like that... people talk. Lots of smoke, visible for miles. Buffalo Boys will be asking questions, trying to find out who lit their fuse. Iron Way, too, if they think one of theirs was involved, or if their rivals suddenly got a lot weaker." He picked up the rag again, meticulously wiping each finger, his eyes still fixed on Tweese, unwavering, like a bird of prey watching a cornered mouse. "Funny thing about that bike, Rider. Aron was talking to Bill last night. Overheard some of it. Mentioned one of their riders went missing a few months back, south of here. Good man, he said. Loyal. Riding a bike just like this one, right down to the fancy leatherwork on the saddlebags. Roses and knights, he said. Real distinctive."

The world seemed to tilt for a moment. Tweese felt the blood drain from his face, a dizzying rush that left him lightheaded. The casual words, delivered with Tuba's almost unnerving calm, hit him with the force of a physical blow. The bike. *This* bike. It wasn't just a random find; it belonged to a missing Iron Way rider. Aron knew it. And Tuba, with his sharp eyes and sharper mind, had clearly put the pieces together. The air in the workshop suddenly felt thick, suffocating. He could hear the distant clang of the blacksmith's hammer, the murmur of voices from the courtyard, but they sounded a thousand miles away. All he could focus on was Tuba's steady, knowing gaze.

"This is a dangerous game you're playing, Rider," Tuba continued, his voice dropping even lower, becoming almost a whisper, though his gaze remained intense, unblinking. "The Iron Way... they ain't easily fooled. They don't forgive mistakes. And they sure as hell don't forgive someone taking what's theirs, or wearing their colors without earning the right." He gestured with his chin towards Tweese's jacket, the heavy leather suddenly feeling like it was searing his skin. "That cog they wear? It means something to them. It means loyalty. It means blood. You ain't got one. And that jacket you're wearing, the one with the pretty flowers? If it's the one Aron thinks it is, they'll want it back. And they'll want to know what happened to the man who was wearing it last. They don't take kindly to loose ends."

Tuba's words were like stones, each one hitting him, shattering the fragile picture he'd built in his mind. The confidence he'd felt after Denver, that dangerous sense of having *earned* the right to this persona, now seemed like a drunkard's bravado in the sober light of morning. An imposter. A thief. He looked down at his own hands, half-expecting to see them stained with something more than just road grime. He wasn't just riding a stolen bike; he was riding a dead man's machine. All the stories he'd heard about the Iron Way being protectors, the ones who cleared the roads… had he just ignored the parts that didn't fit his fantasy? The parts about their brutal justice, the cold, hard pragmatism that kept a gang like that alive? Tuba wasn't painting a new picture; he was just pointing out the details Tweese had chosen to ignore.

"They'll see right through you," Tuba said, his voice flat, devoid of malice, stating it as a simple, undeniable fact. "They'll know you ain't one of them. And when they find out… they'll skin you alive, Rider. Or worse." He paused, then added, his voice barely audible above the distant sounds of the compound, "Especially if they connect you to that mess in Denver. They got no love for the Buffalo Boys, but they don't like loose cannons making trouble in territory they're looking to control. An explosion that big… it draws too much attention. Makes things complicated. And the Iron Way, they don't like complicated."

Tweese felt a wave of nausea, a cold dread that seeped into his bones, making him shiver despite the growing warmth of the day. His grand plan, his dream of trading the bike for a new life in Cheyenne, was a suicidal fantasy. The Iron Way wouldn't welcome him; they'd destroy him. The respect he'd commanded, the good deeds he'd performed in their name, it would all mean nothing to them. Worse, it would be seen as an insult, a dangerous mockery of everything they stood for.

He looked at Tuba, seeing not just a street-smart kid, but a harbinger of a truth he'd been desperately trying to avoid. The boy's young face was serious, his eyes holding a wisdom far beyond his years, a weariness that came from growing up in a world where survival often meant knowing when to keep your mouth shut, and when to speak a hard truth. "Why are you telling me this?" Tweese asked, his voice barely a croak, the words catching in his dry throat.

Tuba shrugged, a small, almost imperceptible movement of his thin shoulders. He finally broke eye contact, looking down at the greasy rag in his hands. "Bill… he's got a soft spot for strays. Says everyone deserves a chance to walk away from a bad hand, if they're smart enough to see the bluff." He looked up again, his gaze direct. "And you, Rider, you got that look about you. Like you're running from something, or maybe running towards something you don't rightly understand." He met Tweese's gaze again. "Consider it a piece of friendly advice. Johnston's Corner is neutral ground, mostly. Bill keeps it that way. But it ain't a place to hide from the Iron Way, not for long. Not if they start looking for you. And they will, if that bike is what Aron thinks it is."

The implications were clear, stark, and terrifying. His time here was limited. His charade was over, or close to it. The confidence he'd felt, the sense of purpose, however ill-founded, that had carried him from Denver, evaporated, leaving behind a hollow ache of fear and profound uncertainty. He felt exposed, stripped bare, the weight of his deceptions pressing down on him.

He spent the next hour in a daze, his mind reeling, replaying Tuba's words, the grim possibilities multiplying with each passing moment. Tuba finished his work on the bike, the engine now running smoother, cleaner than it had since Tweese first found it. The irony wasn't lost on him. The machine that was supposed to be his salvation was now the instrument of his potential doom, a gleaming, powerful beacon that would draw the wrong kind of attention.

He knew he couldn't stay. He couldn't face Aron and Jack-Jack, not now, not with this knowledge hanging over him. He couldn't risk Tuba letting something slip, or the real riders noticing the bike, the jacket, the inconsistencies Tuba had already pointed out. The weight of the truth, and the lies he'd woven, was suddenly unbearable. Every shadow in the courtyard seemed to hold a threat, every unfamiliar face a potential enemy.

He found Bill in the cafe, the older man nursing a cup of coffee, his shotgun leaning against the counter as always. The air in the container was thick with the smell of frying meat and strong chicory. Tweese paid his due for the fuel and the repairs – the last of his scavenged trinkets and a few pre-collapse coins he'd been hoarding – his voice carefully neutral, betraying none of the turmoil raging inside him. He hoped his face didn't look as pale and haunted as he felt.

"Bike's running good," Bill observed, his eyes narrowed slightly, as if sensing the change in Tweese's demeanor, the hunted look that had replaced the weary confidence of the previous day. "Heading out soon?"

"Yeah," Tweese said, avoiding Bill's gaze, focusing instead on a smear of grease on the rough-hewn counter. "Got miles to cover."

"Cheyenne's a long haul," Bill said, his voice even. "Road gets rougher north of here. More patrols, too, the closer you get. Watch yourself, Rider." There was a note of something in Bill's voice – concern? Or perhaps just the weary wisdom of a man who'd seen too many hopeful travelers swallowed by the wasteland. Tweese couldn't tell. He didn't want to know.

Tweese merely nodded, unable to meet the older man's steady gaze. He collected his meager provisions, strapped them to the bike. He didn't seek out Tuba to say goodbye. There was nothing left to say. The kid had delivered his message, a brutal but necessary dose of reality. He had, in his own way, offered Tweese a chance, a warning. What Tweese did with it was his own affair.

He swung his leg over the motorcycle, the familiar leather of the seat offering no comfort now, only a grim reminder of his folly. He started the engine. It purred with a newfound strength, a stark contrast to the weakness and uncertainty that now gripped him. The sound, once a symbol of freedom and power, now felt like a ticking clock.

As he rode out of Johnston's Corner, leaving the fragile sanctuary of its container walls behind, he didn't look back. The road north, the I-25, stretched before him, a grey, indifferent ribbon disappearing into the vast, unforgiving plains. Cheyenne, which had once seemed like a beacon of hope, a destination, now felt like a mirage, a place he could never reach, not as the man he was, and certainly not as the man he had pretended to be.

The motorcycle ate up the miles of broken I-25, its engine now running with a smooth, powerful thrum that was a stark contrast to the turmoil raging inside him. He rode with a grim determination, pushing north, but the destination was now a fractured, uncertain thing, like a reflection in a shattered mirror. The vast, open sky of the high plains offered no answers, only an indifferent expanse that seemed to swallow his anxieties whole, leaving him feeling small and utterly alone.

The bike he rode, the beautiful, powerful machine that had become an extension of himself, was stolen property. Worse, it was the property of a missing rider, a man Aron had called "good" and "loyal." The roses and knights embossed on the leather, which he'd once seen as symbols of a rugged chivalry, now felt like damning evidence, marking him as a thief, perhaps even a murderer in their eyes. The weight of the jacket, which he still wore out of a grim, defiant habit, was no longer a comfort, but a constant, suffocating reminder of his folly. He'd catch his reflection sometimes in the dark chrome of the handlebars, a ghostly figure in black leather, and wonder who he was even looking at.

He rode for what felt like most of the day, the landscape of the high plains unrolling before him in a monotonous panorama of browns and greys. The further north he traveled, the sparser the ruins became, the settlements fewer and farther between. This section of the I-25 was a brutal testament to the limits of the Iron Way's capabilities when faced with overwhelming decay. Sections of the highway were buckled and warped, the concrete slabs tilted at crazy angles like ancient, arthritic bones. He saw where previous, smaller attempts at repair had been devoured by the relentless entropy, crude asphalt fillings crumbling away, leaving even more treacherous edges.

Tweese wrestled with the bike, his muscles straining, his focus fractured between the immediate demands of the treacherous road and the chaotic storm of thoughts in his head. Several times, he nearly lost control as the front tire slammed into an unseen crater or slid on loose scree where the shoulder had crumbled away.

The powerful machine, which had once felt like an extension of his will, now seemed a cumbersome beast, its weight a liability on this decaying artery. Each jolt sent a fresh wave of anxiety through him – not just for his own safety, but for the integrity of the bike itself. If he broke it out here, truly broke it beyond his ability to patch, he was done for.

He was so lost in his dark thoughts that he almost missed it. He'd been riding mechanically, his gaze unfocused, his mind a thousand miles away, replaying scenarios, weighing options that all seemed to lead to ruin. A flicker of movement in the tall grass to his right, a low growl that barely registered over the sputtering of his own engine. He'd let his guard down, his ingrained scavenger's caution dulled by exhaustion and mental anguish. His focus, usually a razor's edge honed by years of solitary survival, had become blunted by the internal cacophony.

Three gaunt shapes emerged from the twilight, low and menacing. Feral dogs, their eyes glowing with a predatory light. They were larger, leaner, and looked far more desperate than the pack he'd helped scare off at Shepherd's Rest. They were on the hunt, and he was isolated, vulnerable, his preoccupation a clear invitation. The lead dog, a scarred brute with saliva dripping from its jaws, its fur matted with old blood and dirt, crept forward, its belly low to the ground, emitting a rumbling snarl that vibrated in Tweese's chest. Its eyes, a pale, hungry yellow, were locked on him.

Then, instinct, or perhaps the lingering echo of the Rider persona – that part of him that had faced down worse things in Denver – took over. With a sudden, explosive movement, Tweese kicked the bike onto its stand, simultaneously yanking the .45 from its shoulder holster. The gun was empty, a useless piece of metal in his hand, but the dogs didn't know that. He stood to his full height, making himself as large as possible, the heavy leather jacket adding to his imposing silhouette, and let out a roar, a savage, desperate sound torn from his own throat, channeling all the fear and fury and despair that had been consuming him.

The effect was startling. The lead dog skidded to a halt, its ears flattening, a flicker of surprise in its hungry eyes. The other two, surprised by the sudden, aggressive display from what they'd likely perceived as easy prey, hesitated, their predatory confidence momentarily broken. Tweese waved the heavy pistol, the setting sun glinting off its dark metal, and took a menacing step towards them, roaring again, a sound more animal than human. He stamped his foot, kicked out a cloud of dust, anything to make himself seem more dangerous, more unhinged than they were.

That was enough. The dogs, creatures of instinct and opportunity, weren't looking for a pitched battle, not against something that fought back with such unexpected ferocity. They were used to prey that ran, or cowered. With a final, frustrated yelp, the leader turned and bolted, its companions scattering into the tall grass, disappearing as quickly as they'd emerged.

Tweese stood there for a long moment, his heart hammering against his ribs, the useless .45 still clutched in his trembling hand. The silence of the plains rushed back in, amplifying the sound of his own ragged breathing. He'd been lucky. Too lucky. His preoccupation had nearly gotten him killed. It was a stark reminder that the wasteland didn't care about his moral quandaries or his shattered illusions. It only cared about survival, and survival demanded constant vigilance. He sank down onto the dusty track, the adrenaline leaving him weak and shaky.

Shaken, he found a defensible spot a little further down the track, a shallow depression ringed by a few gnarled, dead trees, offering at least some cover from the wind and a decent field of view. He made a cold camp, too weary and on edge to risk a fire that might attract more unwanted attention. He ate a little of the food from Johnston's Corner, the jerky tough and tasteless in his mouth, his appetite gone. The encounter with the dogs had stripped away the last vestiges of his brooding. The road north was not a place for philosophical debate or existential crises. It was a place of immediate, brutal realities.

The confidence he'd felt after the events in Denver, the heady, dangerous belief that he'd somehow "earned" the right to the Iron Way persona through his actions, had evaporated like morning mist under a harsh sun. What was he now? He'd struck a blow against the Buffalo Boys, yes. He'd seen true evil and hadn't backed down. He'd felt a spark of something fierce and righteous ignite within him, something that went beyond mere survival. But what did that make him? A vigilante? A madman with a stolen motorcycle and an empty gun? The questions circled like vultures.

He found himself replaying every encounter, every decision. Walsenberg, the feuding farmers, Shepherd's Rest, Bitter Springs... had he done good there? Or had he just been a more sophisticated kind of con man, using the Iron Way's reputation to get what he needed, leaving behind a trail of false hope? The gratitude he'd received, which had once felt like a strange, uncomfortable warmth, now seemed tainted, built on a lie. He remembered Pip's wide, innocent eyes, and a fresh wave of shame washed over him. What would that boy think if he knew the truth?

The temptation to simply turn off the I-25, to find some forgotten dirt track and disappear, was immense. He could ditch the jacket, repaint the bike, become Phil the scavenger once more, a ghost drifting through the ruins, beholden to no one, responsible for nothing but his own survival. It was a life he knew, a life he was good at. Or perhaps, he thought with a flicker of the arrogance that had carried him this far, he could continue the charade on his own terms. Be the Rider he'd pretended to be, a lone agent of rough justice, unallied with any faction, answering to no one but his own newly awakened, if still uncertain, conscience. He could find other struggling settlements, other petty tyrants, other injustices to set right. The idea had a certain romantic appeal, a way to legitimize the changes he felt within himself, to give meaning to the fire he'd started in Denver. But was that just another con, a way to fool himself this time, instead of others?

But the image of Cheyenne, though now tarnished and fraught with peril, still held a stubborn allure. It had been his goal for so long, the promised land at the end of a hard road. And the bike... it was their property. Could he truly claim it, even after what he'd done? Did his actions in Denver, however righteous they felt, give him the right to keep it? The thought of facing the Iron Way, of confronting their reality, was terrifying. But the thought of running, of living the rest of his life looking over his shoulder, felt like a different kind of defeat. He imagined their cold, hard faces, their judgment. He imagined Aron, then the man whose bike he rode, who Aron had called good. What would that confrontation look like? Surrender? A fight he couldn't win?

The nights were cold, the silence of the plains broken only by the cry of a distant coyote or the mournful sigh of the wind. He slept fitfully, his dreams a chaotic jumble of fire, vacant eyes, and the accusing stare of Tuba. The road north became a kind of purgatory, a place of endless, agonizing reflection. He was a man adrift, his compass shattered, his destination uncertain. He was no longer the simple scavenger he'd once been, nor the confident imposter he'd briefly become. He was something else, something new and undefined, forged in the fires of Denver and tempered by the cold truths of Johnston's Corner. But what that something was, and where it would lead him, he had no idea. He only knew that the road ahead was darker, more dangerous, and more uncertain than ever before. And the weight of the jacket, and the stolen motorcycle beneath him, grew heavier with every passing mile.

CHAPTER 9: THE LAST LEG

The plains stretched into a seemingly endless expanse of muted browns and greys, the sky a vast, indifferent canvas that offered neither solace nor judgment. Phillip Tweese rode on, the motorcycle a steady, powerful thrum beneath him, a stark contrast to the chaotic storm of doubt and recrimination that raged within. Tuba's warning had drawn a clear, brutal line in the dust: he was an imposter, and the real Iron Way would see him as nothing more than a thief.

The thought should have been simple, terrifyingly so. But another, more complicated realization kept circling back, refusing to be dismissed. In Denver, when he'd faced that hellish refinery, he'd taken the jacket off. He'd hidden it, shed the skin of the Rider, and walked into that darkness as Phil the crow, the scavenger.

The Rider hadn't seen the boy's murder. The Rider hadn't stared into the vacant horror of that meat grinder. Phil had. And it was Phil's hand, not the Rider's, that had pulled the trigger.

The irony was a bitter pill. All those other times—in Walsenberg, with the farmers, at Shepherd's Rest—he'd been playing a part. He'd worn the jacket, used its reputation as a shield and a key, and performed the role of a hero for his own gain. But the one act of genuine, world-altering, moral outrage? He'd done that all by himself. Without the costume. Without the "permission" the jacket seemed to grant him.

So what did that make him? If his acts of "good" were a con, but his one act of terrible, righteous fury was real, who was he? The thought tangled with Tuba's warning, creating a confusing, maddening knot. The Iron Way would kill him for impersonating one of them, for stealing their property. But the man they would be killing wasn't just the imposter anymore. He was also the man who had, on his own, lit the spark in Denver. Did that matter? To them, no. But to him? He wasn't sure, and that uncertainty was the most terrifying thing of all.

The temptation to simply abandon the quest was a seductive whisper in the lonely wind. He could turn west, into the rugged, broken country that led towards the mountains, lose himself in the wilderness. He could ditch the jacket, alter the bike's appearance, become Phil the scavenger once more, a nameless, faceless survivor answerable to no one. It was a life he understood, a life he was good at. The thought of shedding the crushing weight of his impersonation, the fear of discovery, was almost intoxicating.

Or, a more dangerous, more arrogant thought surfaced: he could become the Rider he'd pretended to be, but on his own terms. He'd seen the power of the symbol, the way people craved order, craved protection. Perhaps he didn't need the real Iron Way. Perhaps he could forge his own legend, a lone wolf dispensing rough justice, a phantom on the broken roads, the man who had actually done the things the jacket only promised. But was that just another, grander con? A delusion born of the violence he'd unleashed?

He was a man adrift, his moral compass shattered, his destination a terrifying question mark. The road north became a blur of introspection, broken only by the necessities of survival – finding meager shelter from the biting winds, rationing his dwindling supplies, nursing the motorcycle over treacherous stretches of decaying asphalt.

It was several days after leaving Johnston's Corner, camped in the lee of a crumbling rock outcropping that offered a meager shield against the relentless prairie wind, that his solitude was broken. He'd built a small, smokeless fire, more for the illusion of warmth and companionship than for actual heat, and was staring into its hypnotic dance when a shadow detached itself from the deeper darkness beyond the firelight.

Tweese was on his feet in an instant, his hand instinctively going to the .45, though he knew it was empty. His heart hammered against his ribs.

A quiet voice spoke from the edge of the light. "Easy there. Just looking for a bit of shared warmth, if you're inclined. Roads are cold."

The figure stepped forward, and Tweese's breath caught in his throat. It was the infiltrator from the Denver refinery, the one whose escape route he had used. Up close, without the grime and the tattered slave rags, the man looked younger than Tweese had initially thought, perhaps in his early twenties. His features were lean, intelligent, his eyes sharp and assessing, holding a calmness that seemed out of place in this ravaged world. He wore simple, durable clothing, practical for travel, and carried a small pack. His name, Tweese would soon learn, was Nate.

"You," Tweese managed, his voice raspy. He lowered the useless pistol slightly, though his stance remained wary. "I saw you. At the refinery."

Nate nodded, his expression unreadable. "And I saw you. You certainly made things… dynamic." A faint, almost imperceptible smile touched his lips. "The fire's not drawing unwanted attention, is it?"

Tweese hesitated. His every instinct screamed caution. This

man was an unknown, clearly capable, and had witnessed Tweese's most desperate, destructive act. But there was something in his calm demeanor, a lack of overt threat, that made Tweese pause. And the shared experience, however brief and chaotic, of the refinery inferno, created a strange, unspoken bond. Besides, the loneliness of the road, the weight of his thoughts, had become a heavy burden.

"Alright," Tweese said finally, gesturing towards the fire with the barrel of the .45 before slowly lowering it completely. "Pull up a rock. Don't have much to offer, but the fire's free."

Nate settled himself on the opposite side of the small blaze, his movements fluid and economical. He didn't seem armed, or at least, not obviously so. For a long moment, they sat in silence, the only sounds the crackle of the fire and the sigh of the wind.

"You travel far?" Nate asked finally, his voice quiet, contemplative.

Tweese grunted. "Far enough. And you?"

"I look for things," Nate said, his gaze distant, as if looking at something beyond the flickering flames. "How things connect. What makes people do what they do. Sometimes you find answers in old ruins, sometimes in new stories."

Tweese snorted. "Not much left to connect out here. Mostly just broken pieces and folks trying not to get stepped on."

"Maybe," Nate conceded. "But even broken pieces can show you the shape of what was. And folks trying not to get stepped on... they make for interesting stories." He turned his gaze directly to Tweese. "You look like you're carrying a hell of a story yourself, Rider. And it ain't a light one."

Nate's words, quiet as they were, landed like a physical blow. The air rushed out of Tweese's lungs. For days, the story had been a toxic, circling brew in his own skull—a chaotic litany of names and faces, of lies and fire. Tuba's knowing eyes, Pip's innocent stare, the dead boy in the refinery. It was a weight that had been pressing down, threatening to crush him. He looked across the fire at Nate, at the calm, assessing gaze that held no judgment, only a quiet understanding, and suddenly the dam inside him broke. The words, tangled and raw, clawed their way up his throat, a confession born not of thought, but of a desperate, overwhelming need to finally let the poison out.

And so, under the vast, star-dusted sky of the high plains, with the small fire crackling between them, Phillip Tweese began to talk. He told Nate everything. The accidental find of the motorcycle and the jacket. The initial cons, driven by a simple need for fuel and food. The way the settlers' expectations had begun to shape him. The growing discomfort, the dawning awareness of a dormant morality. He spoke of the Sanctuary, its efficient, unsettling order. He spoke of Denver, the horrors of the refinery, the dead boy, the white-hot rage that had led him to pull the trigger. He spoke of Johnston's Corner, of Tuba's astute warnings, of the crushing realization that the Iron Way was not what he'd imagined, that his entire journey, his entire hope for a new life, was predicated on a dangerous misinterpretation. He confessed his fear, his confusion, his profound sense of being adrift, his compass shattered.

Nate listened patiently, his gaze never wavering, his expression calm and thoughtful. He didn't interrupt, didn't judge. He simply absorbed the information, an oasis of stillness in the chaotic landscape of Tweese's confession.

When Tweese finally fell silent, the last echoes of his account swallowed by the vast, uncaring night, the only sound was the whisper of the wind and the soft crackle of the dying fire. He felt drained, hollowed out, yet strangely lighter, as if the act of verbalizing the sequence had somehow imposed a fragile order on it. He looked at Nate, expecting... he didn't know what. Condemnation? Pity? Dismissal?

Nate remained silent for another long moment, his gaze fixed on the embers. Then, he looked up, his eyes meeting Tweese's in the dim light. "Yeah," he said, his voice still quiet, but with a thoughtful resonance. "I've heard that story before. Not yours, not all the pieces the same, but the shape of it... a man finds a mask, or a mask finds him, and pretty soon it's hard to tell where one ends and the other begins. Happens more than you'd think."

Tweese frowned. "More than I'd think? Feels like I'm the only fool out here who stumbled into this kind of mess."

"The world's full of messes," Nate said, a faint, dry smile touching his lips. "And full of folks stumbling. Some stumble into a hole and stay there. Some find a way to climb out, or get pushed out, changed. You... you got pushed hard. That refinery... most would have just tried to get clear, find a quiet corner. You threw a rock at the hornet's nest."

"I ain't no hero," Tweese said, the words rough, a familiar refrain even to his own ears now. "I was a con man. A thief. What happened in Denver... that was just... I saw that kid, and something snapped. Could have gotten a lot of people killed, myself included."

"Could have," Nate conceded. "And maybe some did get killed. Big fires like that, they don't pick and choose. But you saw something you couldn't stomach, and you acted. Most folks these days, they see something they can't stomach, they just learn to swallow harder. Or look away. You didn't look away. That's... not common." He paused, his gaze keen. "That kind of reaction, that willingness to risk it all when a certain line gets crossed... that tells a story too."

Tweese was silent, absorbing Nate's words. It wasn't absolution, but it wasn't condemnation either. It was... an acknowledgment. "So what? That makes it right? All the lies, the bike...?"

"Right?" Nate echoed, shaking his head slightly. "Who gets to say what's right anymore, Rider? The Buffalo Boys think they're right. The Iron Way, they got their own laws. Those folks in that big church, they got theirs. Everyone's got a story they tell themselves about why they do what they do." He poked at the fire with a stick, sending a small shower of sparks into the darkness. "My associates… we try to listen to all the stories. Figure out how they fit together, or why they clash. Sometimes, understanding why a man does a thing is more useful than deciding if it was right or wrong."

"Your associates?" Tweese asked, latching onto the phrase. "Who are you people?"

Nate looked up, his expression guarded. "Just some folks who believe that remembering how things were, and watching how things are, might matter. Someday. We try to keep track of things. Information. Useful tech, when we can find it. And people… people who see things a little differently, who don't just go with the flow. People who might have a hand in shaping whatever comes next, for better or worse." He met Tweese's gaze. "Your story, Rider, it's got a lot of those turns in it. A man changing his own path, even if he didn't mean to. That's worth paying attention to."

The wind sighed around them, carrying the scent of dust and distant rain. Tweese felt a strange sense of calm settling over him, a clarity he hadn't experienced in days. Nate wasn't offering easy answers. He was offering a way to look at his own tangled actions without being entirely consumed by guilt or fear.

"So, what now?" Tweese asked, the question raw, stripped of his usual bluster. "That kid at Johnston's Corner… he said the Iron Way will kill me. For the bike. For the jacket. For just being who I am, or who they think I am."

"Tuba's a sharp kid. He knows how outfits like the Iron Way operate," Nate acknowledged, his tone matter-of-fact. "They're organized. They got rules. And they don't like loose ends, or people messing with their reputation or their property. Walking in there, looking like you do, riding that bike... yeah, that's a high-risk play. They're not likely to sit down for a friendly chat first."

The bluntness of it was like a splash of cold water. No comfort there. "So I run," Tweese said, the words flat. "Ditch the bike, the jacket. Disappear. Become a ghost again." It was the sensible option, the scavenger's choice. The path of survival.

"That's one way," Nate agreed. "Safest bet, probably. Live to scavenge another day. Lots of folks choose that way. Nothing wrong with staying alive."

"Or?" Tweese pressed, sensing another, unspoken alternative in Nate's steady gaze.

Nate leaned forward slightly, his eyes reflecting the dying firelight. "Or you ask yourself what that jacket, that bike, means to *you* now. Not to them. Not to those settlers who saw a savior. But to you. What was it that made you stop running your usual game in Bitter Springs? What was it that made you pull that trigger in Denver, knowing what it might cost?"

Tweese thought back. The initial cons, yes, they were for fuel, for survival. But later... the farmers, Agnes, even the disastrous, fiery intervention in Denver... there had been something else. A sense of... an unacceptable imbalance? A feeling that he, Phillip Tweese, had the capacity, and therefore perhaps the obligation, to intervene. A feeling that was terrifying in its implications, in its demands.

"It felt..." he struggled for the words, "...like I couldn't just stand by. Like I had to do *something*. Even if it was crazy." The admission, spoken aloud, felt momentous, a truth he couldn't take back.

"And if that feeling is real," Nate said softly, "if it's not just a fluke, then maybe running isn't the only answer. Maybe the story you're in isn't finished. Going to Cheyenne... it's a gamble, sure.

A long shot. But what if you go, not as an imposter, not as a thief, but as the man who did what he did, for the reasons he did it? Own the story, Rider. See where it leads."

"And they'll kill me," Tweese repeated, the stark reality of it a cold certainty.

"Probably," Nate said again, his gaze unwavering. "But maybe not. Big outfits, they got their rules, but sometimes a man who stands his ground, who speaks his truth even when it's like sticking his head in a noose... sometimes that makes 'em pause. Makes 'em think. Or maybe it just makes 'em kill you faster." He shrugged, a small, almost imperceptible movement. "Point is, what's a conviction worth if you fold the first time it gets really tested? What's the use of seeing a line if you ain't willing to stand on it, even if the ground shakes?"

Nate's words hung in the cold night air. He wasn't telling Tweese what to do. He was laying out the choices, the stakes, with a clarity that was both brutal and strangely liberating. The path of the scavenger, the path of survival, was clear, familiar. Hide, run, forget.

But the other path, the one Nate hinted at... it was terrifying, uncertain, likely fatal if Tuba's assessment of the Iron Way was accurate. Yet, it resonated with a new, stubborn kernel of something within him, something forged in the fires of Denver and validated by this quiet stranger.

"People I know," Nate continued, his voice drawing Tweese from his thoughts, "we watch for moments like these. Moments when someone chooses a hard path, not because it's safe, but because something inside 'em says it's the one they gotta take. Those choices, they tell you a lot about a person. About what might be possible, even in a world like this." He met Tweese's eyes. "A man who acts on what he believes is right, especially when it costs him... that's a rare thing, Rider. A very rare thing. Be a shame if a story like that just... ended in the dirt somewhere, untold, unlearned from."

Nate rose then, his movements as fluid and silent as before. "I've got my own roads to walk, my own things to find. We don't usually cross paths with folks more than once, not out here. But if your road ever leads you to a place where you think your story, your choices, might be worth more than just your own survival... well, some stories have a way of finding the right ears, if they're meant to." He gave a slight nod then. "Think on it, Rider. What kind of story are you writing?"

And then, as silently as he had come, Nate melted back into the darkness, leaving Tweese alone with the dying embers and the crushing weight of his decision.

Tweese sat by the fire for a long time, the young man's words echoing in his mind. *What kind of story are you writing?* He thought of the dead boy. He thought of Pip's trusting face. He thought of the fear in Agnes's eyes, replaced by hope. He thought of the inferno he'd unleashed, a terrible, cleansing fire.

The temptation to run was still strong, a primal instinct. To shed the jacket, the bike, the name, and disappear. But the man who had merely scavenged, who had conned his way through the days, felt like a skin he could no longer inhabit. The things he had done, the lines he had crossed, the lives he had touched – they had coiled around him, a new reality. Nate hadn't offered absolution, nor a guarantee of safety, only a question.

As the first pale light of dawn touched the horizon, Tweese rose. His body ached, and a profound weariness settled deep in his bones, but the frantic storm in his mind had subsided, replaced by a quiet, almost unnerving stillness. He kicked dirt over the last of the embers, the gesture final. He strapped his meager gear to the motorcycle. The engine caught with a steady, powerful roar. He swung his leg over the seat, the leather cool and familiar beneath him. He looked north, down the long ribbon of road disappearing into the horizon. Tuba's warning, Nate's questions, his own uncertain convictions—they weren't behind him. They were up ahead, waiting. His compass was shattered, but the road only went one way for a man who had stopped running. With a slow release of breath, Phillip Tweese – the Rider – pointed the motorcycle north and rode into the gathering light, the roar of the engine a fading echo against the vast, silent plains.

CHAPTER 10: THE COG AND THE RIDER

Kael woke before the first horn, the pre-dawn chill of the high plains seeping through the thick wool blanket in his shared bunkhouse. Around him, the rhythmic breathing of twenty other prospects filled the long, narrow room, a familiar human sound against the distant, mechanical sighs of the compound. He lay still for a moment, listening to the sounds of the Cheyenne stronghold stirring to life beyond the plank walls: the first, hesitant clang of metal from the forges, a rhythm that would soon build to a deafening symphony; the rumble of a heavy vehicle's engine coughing to life in the motor pool; the sharp, clipped barks of the kennel dogs, their excitement a counterpoint to the disciplined quiet of the men. Normal sounds. The sounds of home, of the only world Kael had ever truly known.

But today wasn't normal. Today, the knot in his stomach, usually a dull ache of anticipation for the day's rigors, was tighter, a vibrating coil of nervous energy and a fierce, burning hope. Today, the First Rider would speak. Today, some of them would shed their drab prospect tunics, the color of dust and anonymity, for the black leather of the Way. The thought was a jolt, more potent than the chicory brew that would soon be served.

He swung his legs over the side of his bunk, the rough-sawn

floorboards cold beneath his bare feet, a familiar morning shock. He dressed quickly in the dim light filtering through the narrow, shuttered windows – worn trousers, a patched shirt, the same dun-colored tunic he'd worn for the past year, a garment that felt like a second skin, chafing now with the desire for something more. Soon, perhaps, he'd wear black. The thought sent a shiver down his spine that had nothing to do with the morning chill.

Outside, the air tasted of iron filings and old diesel, a taste as familiar to Kael as the lines on his own calloused hands. The sky was a pale, washed-out grey, the stars fading like dying embers. He joined the trickle of other prospects heading towards the mess hall, their boots crunching on the hard-packed earth, a sound that seemed to echo the grim determination in their young faces.

The compound was a sprawling, utilitarian place, a testament to pragmatic survival built within and around the bones of some massive pre-Collapse industrial site. Concrete pads, vast enough to land one of the old world's flying machines, he imagined, were now cracked and weed-strewn in places, but mostly cleared and utilized. Rusted steel skeletons of forgotten structures, their original purpose lost to time, stood like ancient monuments, interwoven with newer, cruder buildings of scavenged timber, welded shipping containers, and corrugated metal, all enclosed by the formidable outer walls – a patchwork quilt of resilience.

He walked past the motor pool, already a hive of activity despite the early hour. Riders and mechanics, their faces smudged with grease, moved with a practiced, almost balletic efficiency around rows of motorcycles, the air thick with the smell of hot metal, fuel, and the sharp tang of solvents. Voices were low, focused, punctuated by the clang of tools and the hiss of welding torches. Orders were given and obeyed without question, a seamless flow of action. A place for everything, and everyone in their place. That was the Iron Way. Here, there was order. Here, there was a purpose, a visible structure that held the world together.

Further on, he passed the hydroponics sheds, long, low structures covered in patched, translucent sheeting, glowing faintly from within like captured moonlight. Even in this harsh, unforgiving land, where the wind scoured the earth and the sun baked it dry, the Iron Way found ways to make things grow, to provide. He saw figures moving inside, their silhouettes dark against the inner light, tending to the precious crops that supplemented their rations. Beyond them, the rhythmic thud-thud-thud of the water pump, a steady, metallic heartbeat drawing life from deep within the earth, a sound so constant he barely noticed it anymore.

Children, bundled against the morning cold, their faces rosy, were already being herded by a stern-faced woman with a switch tucked into her belt towards the long building that served as the schoolhouse. Their voices were subdued, not the wild shrieks and unrestrained laughter one might hear in a less... structured settlement. They would learn their letters, their numbers, the tenets of the Cog, and the history of the Way – a history of bringing order from chaos, of strength, discipline, and the harsh necessities of survival. Kael had sat in that same schoolhouse, on those same hard benches, learned those same lessons. He remembered the stories of the Before Times, of the Collapse, of the dark years when only the strong, the organized, had endured. The Iron Way had been forged in that darkness.

He saw patrols moving along the inner perimeter walkways, their black leathers stark against the paling sky, rifles slung over their shoulders, their eyes constantly scanning. Their presence was a constant, as much a part of the landscape as the watchtowers or the high walls. Peace had a price, and the Iron Way paid it daily in vigilance and, when necessary, in blood. He'd seen the justice of the Way meted out in the main yard – swift, brutal, and public – for those who threatened that peace, whether from within their own ranks or from the lawless lands beyond. Here, justice was cold, calculated, and, Kael believed with the conviction of the young, necessary. It kept them safe. It kept the chaos at bay. It was the foundation upon which their world was built.

He reached the mess hall, a cavernous, noisy building filled with the smell of chicory coffee, frying fat, and the murmur of hundreds of voices. He took his tray – a thick slab of griddle bread, still warm, a scoop of rehydrated bean mash seasoned with precious salt, a chipped enamel mug of the bitter, hot drink – and found a space at one of long, scarred wooden tables. The talk around him was muted, mostly about the day's work assignments, the state of a particular bike, the ever-present speculation about which prospects would make the cut today. Eyes flickered towards him, towards the other senior prospects, a mixture of curiosity, envy, and perhaps a touch of fear.

Kael ate quickly, the food tasteless in his mouth, his mind elsewhere. He thought of his father, Gareth. Lost on patrol three seasons ago, far afield. Vanished without a trace. A good man, they said. A true rider. If he earned his leathers today, he would be riding the Way in his father's shadow. It was a heavy thought, heavier even than the prospect tunic on his shoulders.

The first horn blew then, its mournful, metallic sound echoing across the compound, cutting through the morning din, signaling the start of the main workday. Prospects began to clear out, heading to their assigned duties – the workshops, the perimeter details, the endless, grinding tasks that kept the Cheyenne stronghold functioning like a well-oiled, if sometimes brutal, machine. But for Kael and the other senior prospects, the horn meant something else. It was time. Time to gather in the main yard, beneath the Warden's tower, and learn their fate.

He rose, his tray clattering on the table, and joined the others filing out into the now brighter morning. The sun was climbing, casting long, sharp shadows across the compound. The metallic taste in the air seemed stronger now, the clang of the forge more insistent, more purposeful. It was the sound of the Iron Way, shaping metal, shaping men. And Kael hoped, with every fiber of his being, that he was strong enough to be shaped in its image, to bear its mark.

He walked with the other prospects, a silent, nervous group, their faces tight with anticipation, towards the main yard. They passed the infirmary, a low, clean building from which came the faint, antiseptic smell of medicinal herbs and something sharper, chemical – a sign of the Way's efforts to preserve life, to mend what was broken, within their own. Order. Even sickness and injury were met with a system here, with skilled hands and hoarded knowledge. They passed the storehouses, great metal sheds, their doors secured with heavy locks, guarded by grim-faced riders. Resources, managed and protected, the lifeblood of their community, not left to chance or the grasping hands of the weak or the opportunistic. This was the strength of the Way, Kael thought, with a surge of fierce pride. Not just the riders and their guns, but this. The ability to build, to maintain, to provide. A stark contrast to the tales of scavengers picking over bones, or settlements starving because they couldn't protect what little they had, or falling prey to the first band of armed thugs that came along.

The main yard opened before them, a vast, dusty expanse dominated by the Warden's tower, its shadow falling long and cool over the assembled prospects. And there, waiting, his black leathers absorbing the morning light, was Aron, First Rider of the Third Wing, his face a roadmap of scars and sun-leathered lines. He paced before them, his boots kicking up small puffs of dust. Jack-Jack, no longer a prospect himself but now a full rider, stood a little behind him, his expression carefully neutral, though Kael caught a flicker of something – sympathy? memory? – in his eyes as Aron's gaze swept over them.

"Today," Aron's voice boomed, cutting through the yard's usual cacophony, which seemed to hush in deference to his presence. "Some of you stop being burdens. Some of you start earning the air you breathe, the fuel you burn." His eyes, pale and hard as winter ice, seemed to pierce each of them in turn. "Some of you will prove you're worthy of the Cog. Others..." He let the word hang, a silent, understood threat. Failure wasn't an option that led to a second chance.

Kael kept his gaze fixed on the Warden's tower, trying to project the calm, unwavering resolve expected of an Iron Way man. Inside, his stomach was a knot of nerves and a fierce, burning anticipation. He'd trained for this his whole life, it felt like. Trained to ride, to fight, to maintain the machines that were their lifeblood, to understand the unwritten laws of their order.

Aron stopped his pacing directly in front of Kael. For a terrifying moment, Kael thought he'd done something wrong, that some infraction, real or imagined, was about to be called out. But Aron's expression, while still stern, held a different quality now.

"Kael, son of Gareth," Aron said, his voice a little softer, though still carrying across the silence that had fallen over the prospects. "Step forward."

Kael's boots crunched on the hard-packed earth as he took two precise steps. He kept his eyes forward, his back straight. He could feel the gaze of the other prospects on him, a mixture of envy and apprehension.

Two other riders brought the motorcycle then, wheeling it out from the main workshop, the morning sun glinting off its polished, dark surfaces. It was a heavy cruiser, powerful, its lines clean and purposeful. Kael had seen it before, of course, in the workshop, being meticulously stripped, cleaned, and reassembled by the best mechanics. It was a beautiful machine, radiating a quiet strength. Beside it, another rider carried the jacket, draped carefully over his arm. Black leather, heavy, intricately tooled with faded roses and thorns around the collar and cuffs, the shoulders reinforced.

Aron gestured towards them. "Your father, Gareth," he began, and Kael's breath caught. His father. Lost on patrol three seasons ago, out towards the Abbey Farm territories. Vanished without a trace. "He was a good man. A true rider of the Iron Way. He rode a bike much like this one."

Kael stared at the motorcycle, then at the jacket. A wave of emotion, hot and sharp, threatened to break through his carefully constructed composure. His father's... He'd been younger, barely into his teens, when Gareth had ridden out for the last time, but he remembered the reassuring weight of his father's hand on his shoulder, the smell of leather and engine oil that always clung to him.

Aron pointed a gloved finger at the jacket. "These were his colors. We recovered this piece from a thief, an outsider who had no right to it." Aron's gaze flicked upwards, towards the western wall of the compound.

Kael's eyes followed, his heart suddenly cold. Against the stark blue of the sky, three tall poles stood silhouetted. Gibbets. From two of them, dark, still shapes hung, picked at by crows. The third was empty, but the ground beneath it was stained. Standard justice for horse thieves, claim jumpers, and those who dared impersonate the Way.

"The man who wore this jacket after your father..." Aron's voice was grim. "He likely had a hand in Gareth's silence. He paid the price for his arrogance. The Iron Way always collects its debts."

Kael looked from the distant, grim figures on the gibbets back to the motorcycle, to the jacket. Which one of those broken shapes had been the thief? Had he been defiant? Had he pleaded? Had he, in his last moments, understood the magnitude of his transgression against the Iron Way, against the memory of a man like Gareth? The questions flickered through his mind, unbidden, unsettling. He pushed them down. It didn't matter. Justice had been served. That was the Iron Way.

"This machine," Aron said, placing a heavy hand on Kael's

shoulder, the gesture surprisingly paternal, "is new, but it is worthy of a son of Gareth. The jacket... it carries his honor." He paused, his gaze intense. "They are yours now, Kael. If you can bear their weight. If you can ride the Iron Way."

Kael looked at the motorcycle, its dark paint gleaming. He reached out a hesitant hand, touched the cool metal of the fuel tank. He could almost feel the thrum of its engine, the echo of his father's hands on the grips. He looked at the jacket, the worn leather, the intricate, faded tooling. It was more than just a machine, more than just clothing. It was a legacy. A responsibility. A heavy, undeniable weight.

He straightened, meeting Aron's gaze, hoping the older man saw not a boy, but a man ready to take his place. "I can, First Rider," Kael said, his voice hoarse but firm. "I will."

Aron nodded slowly, a flicker of something like approval in his eyes. "Good. Then take them. Show us you're worthy of Gareth's memory. Show us you're worthy of the Cog."

Kael stepped towards the motorcycle. As he reached for the handlebars, his fingers brushed against the worn leather of the saddlebags. He knew the stories, the whispers that always circulated among the prospects and younger riders – tales of outsiders and thieves, their cunning and their inevitable, brutal ends when they crossed the Iron Way. Such tales were a constant reminder: an outsider could never understand the Way, and justice for transgressions was swift and absolute.

He swung his leg over the seat. It felt right. He reached for the jacket, the other rider holding it out for him. The leather was heavy, cool against his skin as he slid his arms into the sleeves. It smelled faintly of old oil, of dust from distant roads, and something else... a faint, almost imperceptible scent he couldn't quite place, a ghost of its last wearer.

He settled the weight of it on his shoulders. It was a good fit. A heavy fit. The weight of the Cog. The weight of his father's legacy. The weight of the road ahead. Kael took a deep breath, the taste of iron and diesel suddenly tasting like purpose. He was no longer just Kael, son of Gareth. He was a Rider.

CODA

The fire in the center of the old Walsenberg courthouse common room crackled merrily, sending sparks dancing up towards the soot-stained rafters. Outside, a bitter wind howled, rattling the patched windowpanes, but within the thick stone walls, a fragile warmth held sway. Around the fire, a circle of faces, young and old, glowed in the flickering light, their eyes fixed on the storyteller.

Pip was a man now, his face lined by the sun and the cares of a community that had learned, slowly and painfully, to stand a little taller. His voice, though, still held a hint of that youthful wonder when he spoke of the old days, of the legends that had taken root in the thin soil of their collective memory.

"...and the Rider," Pip was saying, his voice dropping to a conspiratorial hush, though it still carried to every corner of the hushed room, "he didn't ride in and slay monsters for us. That's not how the story goes, not the real way. He came to the granary, and he saw how afraid we were. He saw the broken walls, the neglect. And he didn't just fix it."

A young girl, no more than seven, her chin resting on her knees, piped up, "But he fought the scavs, right?"

Pip smiled, a warm, knowing expression. "No, little one. He did something better. He showed *us* how to fight. He gathered my father, and Samuel, and the others, and he made them see. He showed them how to make the walls strong. He gave them the drums, the chains. He stood with them, in the dark, and when the thieves came, he gave the signal, and it was *our* noise, our shouts, that sent the shadows running. He showed us that the strength to protect this place wasn't in his hands, but in our own."

He paused, letting the image settle. The children's eyes were wide. Even some of the older folk, who had been there, nodded, their expressions reflecting not just awe, but a quiet, enduring pride. The story had been polished by time, its truth found not in a lone hero, but in a shared, awakened strength.

"And he asked for nothing in return," Pip continued, his voice softer now. "Just a little fuel for his magnificent machine, a bike that rumbled like a caged beast. He came like a storm, showed us we didn't have to wait for permission to stand up for ourselves, and then vanished like the morning mist, riding north to wherever the road took him..."

A figure seated in the shadows at the edge of the firelight shifted slightly. He was an older man, his clothes simple, traveler-worn, but of a quality and design subtly different from the homespun garments of the Walsenberg folk. His face, illuminated now and then by a stray flicker of firelight, was calm, his eyes thoughtful, observant. He had listened to Pip's tale with a quiet, unwavering attention.

As Pip finished, a satisfied murmur went around the circle. The legend of the Rider was a comforting one, a reminder that courage wasn't a gift from saviors, but a tool one could learn to wield.

The traveler in the shadows leaned forward slightly, the firelight catching the silver in his neatly trimmed beard. His voice, when he spoke, was quiet, yet it carried a gentle authority that made Pip and the others turn towards him.

"I've heard that story before," the traveler said, his eyes holding

Pip's, a faint, knowing smile playing on his lips. He paused, his gaze distant for a moment, as if seeing not this fire, but another one on a lonely plain. "Not exactly like that, of course. The details shift with the teller, as all good stories do. But the heart of it... the heart of a man stumbling into meaning, and showing others how to find their own... that stays true."

He looked back at Pip, his smile gentle. "Keep telling it. Stories like that... they're like seeds. You never know what they'll grow into."

The traveler leaned back then, melting once more into the shadows, leaving the Walsenberg folk to ponder his words, the crackling fire a warm heart in the cold, dark night, the legend of the Rider a small, defiant spark against the vast, indifferent emptiness of the world.

AUTHOR'S NOTE

Stories are the currency of a fallen world. They are the maps we use to navigate the ruins of what came before and the tools we use to build what comes next. We tell stories about ourselves to survive, and we tell stories about heroes because we need to believe they exist, especially when the world is dark.

Crow and Rider was born from a question: what happens when an ordinary man, a survivor who has forgotten how to be anything else, accidentally steps into one of those hero stories? What happens when the mask he puts on to survive starts to feel like his own skin?

Phillip Tweese's journey along the decaying spine of the I-25 is more than a physical one. It's an exploration of the space between who we are and who we pretend to be, and the often blurry line that separates a con man from a savior. It's a story about the power of symbols, and how the legends we create can sometimes create us in return.

This novel is set in the Iron Way world, a rich and compelling post-apocalyptic landscape first imagined by C. Holtorf, whose creation was an invaluable spark for this particular tale.

Thank you for taking this ride. I hope the story stays with you, long after you've turned the final page.

—Max Sterling

www.ingramcontent.com/pod-product-compliance
Lightning Source LLC
Chambersburg PA
CBHW052006240626
47153CB00008B/2765